Bury the Garden

Tahlia Campbell

The Rural Publishing Company

The Rural Publishing Company
Website: https://theruralpublishingcompany.com.au
Email: hello@theruralpublishingcompany.com.au

Prologue

The moment she died she felt a nothingness that terrified her more than any hell she could have imagined.

Inky blackness on all sides, with nothing to ground her. There was no weight to her, no sensation at all. She couldn't see, couldn't hear, couldn't feel, couldn't talk. What would she even say? Would she cry out for help? From who?

At least there was no pain. That was the one thing that made her sure she was not in hell. But maybe this was worse. Being suspended in total darkness, feeling nothing. Imagine drowning in the deepest part of the sea, but you couldn't feel the coolness of the water or even your own heart pounding as it tries to keep you alive. There's no tether to the world or your own body.

She tried to think. She thought she was panicking, but could she feel emotions anymore? There was no physical sign of this, no tensed muscles or shortness of breath. Just her thoughts.

Whose thoughts?

She scrambled to grab hold of a memory, but there were none. She couldn't recall her name, what she looked like, or even how she died. Her life was as blank as the empty space around her.

Something parted the darkness, a single shining star in the midnight sky. A tiny tear in space, so far in the distance then suddenly right in front of her. A sharp, pointed claw pierced through the blackness and tore downwards, creating a tear. Painfully bright light flooded her senses and her world became one of pain. That vast, incomprehensible void that made up her being was pulled into some form of 'self', which was in turn ripped unceremoniously into the rift.

Not alive, but not as dead as she might have been.

Chapter One

ANOTHER DAY OF SCROUNGING through objects that might give her a taste of what it was like to be alive. Olive scoped out the various stalls, scanning through the crafts, homemade trinkets and organic food. This market came around every month, and it was mostly an opportunity for local families to make money off the clutter that had been blocking their garage for years.

Most of those things were useless to Olive – plastic and metal weren't what she needed. She walked past stalls selling used books, candles and jewellery, before she found a box of cassette tapes that stopped her in her tracks. Pausing without getting too close, she inspected the tapes, looking for a title that might spark a memory. Her brow furrowed. She recognised a few of the bands' names, but only from her previous hunts at thrift stores and other markets. None of them meant anything to her. She let out an exasperated sigh, blowing a lock of auburn hair away from her face.

'Looking for anything in particular?'

She jumped at the sound of a voice. She had forgotten that she was visible now. The man who had spoken was older, with greying hair and an unshaven face. He wore a plain navy polo shirt and dirty jeans, and he stood in a wide stance with his arms crossed. He might have been intimidating, but his eyes seemed tired and bored. It was unusually warm for autumn, and everyone at the market was in a drowsy, sun-induced stupor.

Olive slid her hand under the sleeve of her rust-coloured sweater and pushed it up over her elbow. She could see the man was sweating. She should have been too, if the heat had any effect on her. She smiled quickly, politely, careful not to glance at him too long. 'No, thank you. Just browsing.'

The man shrugged. 'Let me know if you see anything you like.'

Olive nodded, letting her gaze wander over his wares for a few seconds before slowly turning away from his stall.

She heard a cough behind her and whirled around. Rita in her leather jacket and boots stood next to her, and tugged her arm. 'Come on, don't get distracted. Let's just get what we came here for, then we can relax.'

Olive threw another furtive glance back at the man's stall. 'Cassette tapes were big in the '80s, right? Did the '90s have them, too?'

Rita rolled her dark eyes in amusement. 'God, I don't know. I stopped keeping track of history about a decade after I died.'

'You're no help at all,' Olive shoved her, but she was smiling. Rita lifted a dark hand to her head and pushed her back, gently.

'You don't really think you're going to get your memories back by looking at all this old stuff, do you?' Rita raised one eyebrow high. She was teasing, but there was an underlying concern.

Olive huffed and pulled away, loosening another lock from her ponytail and twisting it around her finger. 'It's worth a shot, isn't it? That's what they try with amnesia patients, jogging their memories with things from their pasts. That's all I'm trying to do.'

Rita shook her head, the tight curls of her textured hair swaying slightly around her face. 'You've been talking to Ezekiel too much.' Ezekiel was another ghost. He had been studying to be a psychologist when he died, and when he'd learnt that Olive didn't remember anything about her life, he was determined to help her solve the mystery of her past. 'You're not a regular amnesia patient, Olly. You're dead, which means there's probably some cosmic force at work. It's more than just your brain that's causing this.'

Olive tilted her head with narrowed eyes. 'So you're saying it's my *soul* that's messed up?'

Rita fixed her with a look. 'Don't get all huffy on me, girl. I'm just saying, don't get your hopes up looking at tapes. If we finish this job, you'll get to experience your life first-hand.'

Yes, that was the reason they were here. Find the tokens, return them, and earn their way back to their lives. Olive nodded reluctantly and took Rita's arm. They walked around the market, not stopping at any particular stall but passing their eyes over every item on display. Eventually Rita elbowed Olive and subtly pointed to a table laid with wooden carvings of animals. The token there caught Olive's eye immediately, as they always did. This one was a carving of an owl perched on a gnarled tree branch, the feathers around its eyes forming angry eyebrows. It glowed the amber colour of the tokens Olive had been collecting for the entire span of her memory.

These tokens, according to the spirit who requested them, had been stolen from the earth, and by returning them, Olive and Rita were holding up their end of the deal that would grant them life again. Olive could never work out what made one token different from everything else. Surely all of the wood carvings were the same? But the spirit always wanted something specific, and they wouldn't know what it was until they saw it.

Olive and Rita shared a glance, and Olive nodded. She smiled brightly at the lady behind the table and pointed towards the owl. The sticker in front of it declared the price to be $5. 'I'll take this one, please.'

The lady, with long grey hair and world-weary eyes, smiled painstakingly in response to Olive's cheery expression. 'Good choice. This one's special, he'll bring you luck.'

Olive handed over the coins, careful not to make contact with the woman's leathery skin, and gave another pleasant grin. 'I sure hope so.'

Olive took the owl without waiting for a bag, and watched the women put the coins in a biscuit tin. Those would disappear in a few hours; they were illusions that the spirit had granted them to make the job easier. They could always just steal the tokens – after all, the ghosts could disappear from the sight of the living – but buying them instead gave Olive the chance to interact with people, explore the world and get a sense of what it would feel like to be alive.

Out of the corner of her eye, Olive caught someone staring at her – a young man her age, maybe younger, with a mess of dark hair. He looked sullen and out of place in the market, and as soon as he realised she'd noticed him, he looked embarrassed and turned away. Olive watched him carefully, and he kept sneaking glances when he thought she wasn't looking.

'Looks like you've got an admirer,' Rita chimed, her voice low in Olive's ear.

Olive laughed and tossed her hair back. 'Can you blame him?'

Rita rolled her eyes and Olive wanted the conversation to end there, but there was something in the boy's eyes that made her uneasy. 'You don't think he's …'

'What, a hunter?' Rita clicked her tongue. 'Don't think so. They're usually more confident, and even if he was one, he'd be carrying a weapon if he was on the job. I don't think we need to worry.'

Rita hummed contentedly as they walked. 'That went well. One of the easier ones we've had. Hey, remember when that woman was wearing a token on a necklace –'

'And we had to run and buy a necklace to trade with her?' Olive recalled, chuckling softly at the memory. 'Yeah, I remember.'

'She did *not* want to give that thing up,' Rita chuckled, her voice as low as a motorcycle's hum. 'She looked like we were trying to mug her!'

Olive giggled lightly, running her thumb over the carvings in the wooden owl. The details were exquisite. It almost looked real.

Rita finished her laughing with a long exhale. 'Alright, amnesiac, you got anything else you want to look at before we take this thing back?'

Olive hummed, looking back over the market. Now that they had recovered the token, all the magic had faded. The sky seemed more grey, the golden glow of the sun hidden behind clouds. 'I think I'm good. Let's head back so we can celebrate.'

Rita grinned, stretching her arm across Olive's shoulders and rubbing her arm excitedly. 'That's what I like to hear.'

Getting around was fairly easy as a ghost. It didn't matter where they were, they could always find their way back to the spirit if they wandered far enough. The scenery of the market and the surrounding oak trees dressed in orange slowly began melting into each other, forming an endless forest. Eventually, the little insect-like sprites began flitting around, and Olive could spot the creatures she called fairies in her own mind. They weren't really fairies, that implied something much nicer than what they really were. They used to be ghosts, like Olive and Rita, who made the same pact with the forest spirit. But these fairies had gone too long without collecting enough tokens, and had started losing their grip on humanity. They steadily gained animalistic features, like sharp teeth, claws, yellow eyes, which then progressed into pointed ears and tails, until eventually they were entirely animal.

There were three in particular that Olive had gotten used to. They were at an unsettling in-between stage, where they still had human posture and hair, but their faces had changed enough that they looked like they were wearing disturbingly realistic animal masks. The three girls were a small blonde with a rabbit face; a tall, broad brunette with antlers; and a burly dark-haired girl with pointed fox-like features. They stuck together as an inseparable trio, cheerful and friendly with a spark of mischief. Despite the differences in their forms, they seemed to move as one and the way they spoke was almost like one person with three voices, each thought building on the last but not independent.

The rabbit girl waved at Olive with a clawed hand, and Olive waved back, a little hesitantly. The trio watched from a distance, their cold black eyes tracking the two ghosts as they ventured further into the forest. Olive knew by now that this forest, once it morphed away from whatever location they'd come from, was part of the spiritual world, the realm of ghosts. It was a space that existed everywhere and nowhere, alongside the realm of the living but apart from it.

The forest spirit was always in the same place whenever they were needed. A clearing in the forest, with an oak tree standing tall beside a stream, surrounded by toadstools. They were sometimes tending to plants and animals, and sometimes they split from the oak tree itself, as if they were nothing but a bit of bark peeling away. They had no name, no gender, no age, but they took amusement in being called Gaia. Olive could see them now, painting moss up the side of a tree with their fingers. In the vaguest sense possible, Gaia could be described as an angel. They had wings; giant wings that stretched even higher than their own tall frame, but the feathers weren't all white. They were like a quilt of mismatched colours, some black like a crow's, some speckled like a barn owl's, others iridescent like a duck's. Their dress was made out of moss and lichen, with fungus and flowers growing and bugs crawling. Below where the sleeves ended, the arms were bone, and the dress seemed to grow out of the ground, moving with it instead of on top of it. Their skin was brown and textured like the bark of the oak, and their hair was thick tendrils of vines and leaves twisted together.

Their face was inscrutable, covered by a giant skull that looked like it could have belonged to some kind of canine. Their eyes, when visible through the skull, were a vibrant green, and they turned them on the girls now.

'Ah, you've brought a treat for me, have you?' They spoke in a voice that sounded of insect wings and crunching leaves. 'Let me see it.'

Olive stepped forward, holding out the owl towards them. They took it with a skeletal hand, and Olive shivered where it touched her skin. A sound like purring, or maybe the buzzing of insects, emanated from Gaia as they inspected it. They turned around and reached up into the tree behind them, placing the owl on a steady bough. They turned back to the girls, their barely visible mouth turned up into a warm smile. Olive watched as the owl slowly began to morph into the tree, losing its defining features and melding with the tree until it looked like it had never been anything different.

'Beautiful, isn't it?' Gaia said. 'Thank you, girls. I can't blame mortals for wanting to keep parts of nature for themselves, but they need to realise that the planet does not belong to them.'

Olive was impressed by Gaia's restraint. If she were a powerful forest spirit, she'd be pissed off at all of the damage that humans have done to the world. But it seemed like Gaia's powers were limited, which explained why they needed to recruit dead people to get what they want.

'I suppose you'll be wanting your rewards, then?' Gaia asked, a twinkle in their voice. They extended each of their hands towards the girls, palms up, and from them emerged two glowing balls of pale yellow light, like a firefly the size of an apple.

Olive eagerly reached for the one closest to her, not bothering to wait for Rita. She cupped the flickering ball of light in her hands and revelled as she pushed it into her chest, feeling a warm tingle spread from her heart through her entire body. With this light came sensation. She felt the humidity bearing down on her, and the little balls of sweat forming on her skin were like a blissful shower. Under her feet, the grass grew tall, and flowers bloomed. She felt the wind blowing in her hair, she smelled the moss and the decaying leaves of the forest. She felt her breath move through her lungs; it sustained her, nourished her. She felt it stream through her body. She felt her heart beating in her chest and the itching of her eyes that made her blink. She felt *alive.*

But until they had collected enough tokens, it would only ever be a feeling. This was the reward for reclaiming what was taken from the earth, but it didn't last forever. The next morning would come and they would go back to being empty. Detached from the world. Olive looked over at Rita, who was laughing joyously with her eyes closed, holding her arms out to the wind and letting the crisp leaves run through her fingers. She coughed a few times, a hearty, rasping cough, but she didn't seem to mind. Sparks flickered from her fingertips until they grew into small flames in the palms of her hands, their warmth emanating all the way to Olive.

Placing two fingers on her wrist to enjoy the novelty of having a pulse, Olive looked back at Gaia, who was starting to turn away. 'So, how many more of these things do we have to collect?'

Gaia's head jolted towards her, their eyes a flash of pale green in the darkness behind their skull mask. 'What do you mean?'

Olive saw Rita frown at her out of the corner of her eye, but she ignored her. 'I mean, how much longer are we going to keep doing this before you hold up your end of the deal?'

Gaia stepped towards them again, wings raised up high, and Olive became acutely aware of how inhuman they were. 'You'll keep collecting them until I decide you've done enough.'

Rita elbowed Olive sharply and hissed, 'Cut it out, Olly.'

But Olive wasn't finished yet. She felt she had to clear her throat to speak again, and she coughed with less vigour than Rita had. 'And when exactly will that be? We've been doing this for God knows how long, and it doesn't seem like we're any closer to getting our lives back. And you *still* haven't explained why I'm the only one who doesn't have my memories.'

The bugs crawling around Gaia's form suddenly scurried upwards, disappearing into their hair. The feathers in their wings ruffled individually. They towered impossibly high over the girls as the forest grew silent. Olive took a step backwards instinctively, but Gaia stayed as still as the old oak tree they had stepped out of. Olive could see the faint glow of their green eyes as they fixed their gaze on her.

'That,' came the scratchy voice, 'is not my decision to make. I don't want to keep you here any longer than you need, but you don't have another option. Unless, of course, you want to end up like them,'

A skeletal finger pointed to the trio of fairies, still watching the girls. The deer turned her head away, and the rabbit scratched behind her tall ear with her claws, but the fox's eyes didn't waver. Olive's stomach twisted in disgust, which was a rare and unsettling feeling.

Rita hooked an arm around Olive's elbow, pulling her backwards. She shot Olive a glare, then looked at Gaia with steady confidence. 'We understand. We'll be back with the next token soon.'

Gaia lowered their head in what might have been a nod, and silently turned from the girls, shutting them out. Their wings shrouded their form, then they vanished into a cloud of mismatched feathers.

Chapter Two

Rita adjusted the collar of her jacket as she overtook Olive on the path. She coughed again, and then Olive could smell it, the scent of tobacco flowing from her breath into the wind blowing in her direction. Rita had mentioned that she'd smoked when she was alive, but that wasn't what killed her. No, she had died in a motorcycle accident, with her girlfriend on the back behind her. Her girlfriend had survived, miraculously, but Rita hadn't. The way she told it, she wasn't too upset about the circumstances of her death. As a black trans lesbian living in the 50s, there were a lot of worse ways she could have died.

Olive both loved and hated hearing about Rita's life. She lived vicariously through Rita's memories, learning about the world as it was over 60 years ago. Even if the information was outdated, Olive ate up every detail she could. At the same time, she was envious of a life she'd never known, and Rita's experiences wouldn't have had much overlap with her own. Olive, in her life, would have experienced the world as a white bisexual woman in the 80s and 90s, so she couldn't imagine herself living Rita's life.

Learning about the positive aspects of Rita's life was also painful. It hurt to know that she was being denied all her memories, good and bad. Did she have a partner? Were they still alive, and missing her? What about her family? It felt like she was being punished, but she wasn't sure what for.

Rita continued through the forest, Olive trailing behind her. The way back to their house was the same way that they found Gaia every time; they just kept walking, and it revealed itself eventually.

As the house began to take shape in the distance, Rita sighed heavily and stopped in her tracks. She waited for

Olive to catch up, then without looking at her, said 'Why did you have to do that?'

Olive blinked, then squared her shoulders, tensing her arms. She stared at the ground. 'I wanted answers. Why should we have to keep guessing? Gaia's just using us to get to whatever agenda they have planned.' She took a deep breath and spoke softly. 'I need to know who I was before I go back.'

Rita looked at her over her shoulders, her eyebrows puckered in pity. 'You still think they're going to send us back? I figured at this point there's no way they were telling the truth.'

Olive frowned. The recent gift of temporary life she'd been given was making the blood rush to her face, her cheeks burning. 'Why would I not believe them? That's the whole reason we're here, so that we can go back!'

'I get that, but reversing death? That's some reality-warping shit. And I don't think Gaia's in charge, exactly. They're just a spirit, there's got to be someone else. God or whatever –'

The wind picked up around Olive as she clenched her fists in frustration. 'What other choice do I have?'

Thistles sprung up from the ground around Olive's feet, a side-effect of her anger aided by the abilities granted to her by Gaia. 'You heard what they said. If we stop finding tokens, we'll turn into monsters, or animals, or whatever it is they are. But I don't have anything else! You *know* that. I showed up in the forest with no memories and nothing to go on except for the hope that I'd get to go back to my old life. If I can't believe in that, I have nothing.'

Rita watched her for a while, scanning her heavy breathing and the leaves spinning hastily around her. She sighed, and curls of grey-blue smoke crept out of her mouth. 'I'm sorry, Olly. I know. I know you really want this. I just can't help thinking ... what if they're lying to us? What if they're never going to let us go?'

'Don't *you* want to go back? For Carla?'

Rita clenched her jaw. 'The way I see it, me dying is just the way things were meant to be, you know? If I went back, it would change a lot of things. Of course I'd love to see her again, stop her from getting hurt the way she did. But even *if* Gaia is lying? I'm fine with staying here, finding tokens for however long they need. The world today isn't perfect, but it's better than when I was alive. Better for people like me, in some ways.' she sighed again. 'I wish I could help with your memories. I really do. I just think you need to be ok with the idea that you might not get them back.'

Olive lowered her gaze, the thistles surrounding her beginning to wilt. 'It's different for you. At least you have *something* to cling to. If we end up serving Gaia for eternity, you still know who you were before this. I don't *have* anything else. If I can't believe that I'll come out of this with more of myself than what I started with, I don't have any reason to save myself.'

The pity was back in Rita's eyes, and Olive hated it. Rita gently brushed her fingers against Olive's forearm. 'Let's not worry about this right now, okay? We're alive, for now at least. We've got a bottle of wine, we've got good music, let's make the most of it!'

Olive let herself smile and leaned into Rita as she put a leather-clad arm around her shoulders. The trees started melding back into familiar territory and became more solid. The woods where Olive and Rita's house was situated stood apart from the spiritual realm, but the houses were invisible to the living. They used to be real, physical buildings, but they had become decrepit over time and the earth had reclaimed them. Gaia was able to recreate them, but they belonged to the ghosts, a liminal space caught between life and death. Rita and Olive's house – probably closer to a log cabin – was situated near a small farm, with a tiny flock of sheep, a cow, and a dog. The house had two stories, but most of the first floor was one room. A small kitchen was in the corner, with most of the space taken up by a wooden dining table and chairs. Upstairs was the bathroom and two bedrooms. Olive and Rita spent a lot of time in both rooms, but Olive's bedroom was special to her. Rita obviously couldn't bring anything back from her old life, but she was specific in what she bought into the room. Motorcycle magazines, movie posters from the 50s, sci-fi novels, and collectable bottle caps littered her room, as well as some modern trinkets that had caught her eye.

Olive's room wasn't as purposeful. Based on the era she would have grown up in, she had collected as much miscellaneous 80's and 90's memorabilia as she could get her hands on. Most of them were toys, some movies and trashy romance novels, but nothing seemed significant to her. In her bad moods, her collections seemed to mock her, a statement to the things she *should* remember but couldn't. Besides the useless puzzle pieces of her past, there were empty wine bottles scattered on the ground, some newspapers, although they were hard to come by, and jars full of coins, feathers and flowers. She kept a sketchbook and some charcoal sticks on the desk facing the window, which let the golden sunset into the room and gave it an amber haze like the glow from the tokens. Pages from the sketchbook were torn out and tossed on the floor in her frustrations. Ezekiel had told her that drawing could be useful in working out problems, maybe even recovering memories, but every time she failed to remember, she'd become distressed.

A little deeper into the woods was another house that belonged to Ezekiel and Marcus. Their house looked more like you would expect one inhabited by ghosts to look; all dark paint and a tall roof with cathedral-like windows and a couple of gargoyles on top. It was simple on the inside, its many hallways and rooms mostly bare except for the Gothic furniture sparingly placed around. Olive hadn't seen either of the boys' rooms, but she could venture a guess as to what was in each of them. Ezekiel's would have shelves full of Gothic literature and journals from all the best psychologists of the past century. He'd probably have a few playscripts as well. Marcus's would be full of music sheets and books written about famous composers.

His grandparents – or maybe great-grandparents, Olive couldn't remember – had been Spanish immigrants, and he had explained that English was his first language, that he hadn't started learning Spanish until he was a teenager, but music was something everyone understood. He didn't talk about his death as much as the others, but Olive knew that he had drowned sometime in the 70s. Ezekiel had died on his way to college in the 60s. His bus had driven over a bridge that had started to collapse. Neither of them went into much detail about their lives, maybe because it hurt them to talk about what they'd left behind, the decades they were denied, but Olive was secretly grateful for it. She wanted to spend time in their company without feeling like they wished they were somewhere else.

Olive and Rita arrived at the boys' house after passing their own. The door was open, as it usually was, and Ezekiel and Marcus were sitting in the dark dining room. Marcus sat on the floor playing his guitar, his dark hoodie tied around his waist, revealing the tattoo of a sparrow on his forearm. Ezekiel was seated at the table, his eyes closed underneath his wire frame glasses. They both looked up as the girls entered, Marcus greeting them with a bright grin.

'You two are looking lively!' He said, carefully placing his guitar on the table before jumping up to give them both a hug. Olive relished in it, feeling the warmth of his body envelope her.

Rita laughed, moving to pull Ezekiel's thin frame into an embrace. 'Please tell me you found a token, too,'

Ezekiel nodded, his curly hair bobbing. 'We sure did. It wasn't easy, though. Someone else was already planning on buying it, and the shopkeeper wasn't too happy that we had to pay him in coins. I don't think I'll ever get used to those plastic cards.'

By this point Olive was already in the kitchen, climbing on top of the countertop to get to the cabinet. Inside were rows of bottles of wine and whiskey, saved up from all the years they'd been dead. Gaia usually only gave them enough magic for the coins they'd need to buy one token, but every now and then the ghosts were able to haggle a good bargain for themselves and had some left over. Olive noted bitterly that it was like they were being given an allowance. She scanned the labels of the bottles, looking for a good red. She found one from 1985 and took it down with her. Holding it by the neck with a wolfish grin, she strolled back into the dining room and looked around. 'Let's have a drink, shall we?'

Ezekiel went to grab glasses, and Olive popped the cork. She took a large swig from the bottle and handed it over to Rita, who shook her head with a bemused scoff when she saw the year. The four of them gathered outside, grabbing some food from the boys' kitchen. It was a little stale, but it didn't matter, not when they weren't able to taste it.

They laid out on the grass amongst the crisp leaves. Olive took out the small cylindrical packet of Lifesavers she'd slipped up the sleeve of her sweater at the market. Rita laughed, her eyes wide with disbelief, but she said nothing about it. It was a little thing, really, and no one was likely to notice. Even if they did, they'd never catch her.

Ezekiel poured the glasses and passed them around. 'Had any luck with the memories, Olive?'

Olive rolled her eyes and took another big swig. 'What do *you* think? No, my mind is still as blank as my new sketchbook.'

'She's handling it well,' Rita muttered sardonically. 'Managed to piss of Gaia today,'

Marcus and Ezekiel's eyes widened, and Olive glared at her in irritation. 'I didn't piss them off, ok? I just wanted answers.'

'That's fair. I would too if I were you,' Marcus shrugged, but Ezekiel's eyebrows drew together in concern.

'You really shouldn't provoke them. We have no idea what they're capable of, and besides, I'm sure there's a perfectly logical explanation for your missing memories. We just have to –'

'You don't get it,' Olive snapped, feeling frustration bubbling in her chest. '*None* of you get it. Do you know how frustrating it is to not know anything about myself, and not even know *why?* It's like I'm serving a sentence for a crime I can't remember committing.'

The other three ghosts glanced around at each other, avoiding Olive's eye. She had dug the fingers of her free hand into the dirt beside her, and thorny vines began crossing over her hand. Finally, Ezekiel spoke up. 'You're right, Olive, we don't understand. And there might not be much we can do about it, but ...'

He hesitated, chewing his lip. 'There's something else we can try, if you want to. We could try hypnosis therapy.'

Marcus let out a laugh. 'Really? Hypnosis? That's not actually a thing, right?'

Ezekiel heaved a deep sigh, running a hand through his curls. As much as they loved each other, Marcus really knew how to push his buttons. 'Yes, Marcus, it is a thing. It's probably not what you're thinking of, with a swinging pocket watch. Psychologists have used it for years to kind of ... unlock memories that have been blocked by trauma.'

'Would that work on me, though? If we don't know what the trauma is that caused it?'

'It's hard to say. Of course, we could be dealing with something magical that's entirely out of our control, but ...'

The three gazed at Olive expectantly. She let her head slowly flop to the side, the red wine making her mind hazy. 'No offense, Zeke, but I think it sounds dumb.'

Rita put her hand on Olive's, pulling away some of the vines. 'Getting your memories back is literally all you've spoken about today. Isn't worth a shot? I mean, it's not like you've got anything to lose.'

Olive groaned and leaned heavily against Rita, almost sloshing the wine out of her glass. 'Mm ... ok. Tomorrow, though. We're having fun tonight.'

Marcus pulled out his guitar, and Ezekiel poured another round of drinks. Olive felt a buzz in her mind and a warmth flowing through her as the alcohol took hold, blurring her thoughts and wrapping her in a feeling of sleepy bliss. The four ghosts soaked in the setting sun, singing along to the guitar and swaying. Hours passed in a haze. Olive had ended up with her head in Rita's lap, Rita's dark fingers trailing through red hair, and Ezekiel's head rested against Marcus's shoulder as he continued to play. Olive soaked in as much of the evening as she could, knowing it wouldn't last.

It seemed like there was no time at all before Olive's head snapped up at the sound of leaves crunching. Marcus stopped strumming and the four of them went silent. There was a humanoid silhouette amongst the trees. The ghosts froze, then Rita picked up a rock and threw it just short of where the noise had come from. The shadow jolted back behind a tree, letting out a small yelp. Its voice sounded young.

Olive stood up slowly, taking a few steps forward. She held up her hands as a sign of peace. 'It's ok, you can come out,' she said, like she was coaxing a wild animal. 'We're not going to hurt you.'

She heard Marcus snickering behind her. She must have been slurring her speech, and she was probably swaying with tipsiness.

They waited in silence for a few seconds, Rita rising to stand next to Olive. It wasn't long before a figure stepped out of the shadows, and they all breathed a sigh of relief. It was a human figure, a new ghost. Olive had been right; the person was young. They looked to be sixteen or seventeen, a few years younger than Olive was. They stood timidly, half-covered by the tree. From what Olive could see, they had long, silky black hair under a woollen beanie. They had Asian features, rich golden-brown skin and a few freckles. Their wide-set form wore a baggy sports shirt in an off-white colour with bright green and yellow stripes on the sleeves and collar, as well as ripped jeans and beat-up sneakers. They slowly, cautiously stepped forward, careful to keep their distance. They raised up one hand in an awkward wave. 'Um ... sorry for crashing your party.'

Olive laughed in relief. 'Oh, don't worry about it! Why don't you come join us? Tell us your story.'

She beckoned them forward, but still they hung back a bit. They seemed to relax slightly though, their shoulders dropping. 'Sounds like it could be fun. I'm Jay, and uh

...' they paused, looking closely at each of the ghosts. 'My story, well ... I don't think I have one? I mean, this is the most realistic dream I've ever had, but I just kind of ended up here. Not much else to say.'

Olive frowned, meeting eyes with Rita. She turned back to Jay. 'A dream? Is ... is that what you think this is, honey?'

Jay's face froze. Their eyes darted to the side. 'Y-yeah, I mean ... the last thing I remember was going to bed, and then I ended up in this forest.' They looked around. 'This is near the Murphy farm, isn't it? I know this place, I used to come here with my family when I was little.'

'But ... you didn't see Gaia when you got here? They didn't explain what was going on?' Ezekiel asked.

Jay tilted their head. 'Gaia? Like in Greek mythology?'

Rita crossed her arms, leaning her weight onto her right leg. 'This is something different. Something weird is going on here.'

Olive tugged on her hair. 'You think this is a dream, so ... you don't remember how you died?'

The look on Jay's face was one of pure terror. Their eyes widened and they stumbled back a few steps while Olive felt the sickening feeling that something was very wrong. Jay glanced around fervidly, clutching at the collar of their shirt. 'No ... no, I can't be dead! I survived! I've been fine this whole week!'

'What do you mean, you survived?' Ezekiel asked carefully.

Jay looked down at their hands and began pinching the skin between the thumb and forefinger. 'Last week I was camping with my brother, and there was a storm and a tree fell onto my tent ... at least, that's what everyone's been telling me. I don't remember it, the doctors said I have amnesia from the tree hitting my head.' They looked down at their body. 'Why aren't I in any pain? My legs were broken, I ... oh god, I really am dead, aren't I?'

Olive could see the terrified look in Jay's eyes, even as the word 'amnesia' echoed in her head and sent her mind into overdrive. She moved closer to them and went to put a hand on their shoulder, but it phased right through. They looked a little frightened, but it confirmed the thought that was already forming in Olive's head. 'Hey, hey, don't worry. I don't think you *are* dead. That's not how things usually work around here, is it?'

Ezekiel shook his head and stood up, too. 'If you *had* died, you should have either met Gaia straight away or just ... passed on to whatever comes after this. Unless you died in your sleep ...' he trailed off, cupping his chin with his hand in thought.

'What are you thinking?' Marcus asked.

'I don't know ... it's possible that a near-death experience like that could allow you to see the spiritual realm in your dreams. You know, like your consciousness is stuck between the two planes.'

Marcus chewed his lip. 'Should we ask Gaia? They'd probably know.'

'Who *is* Gaia?' Jay asked, their voice trembling and rising in pitch.

'Gaia is a forest spirit, a powerful elemental.' Ezekiel explained. 'Sometimes, spirits are caught between life and death and can't pass on, and they can become trapped. But Gaia offered us a choice. We help them get what they want, and they help us.'

Olive noticed how he kept the description vague. She watched the gears turning in Jay's mind, and they just seemed more confused.

Rita coughed harshly, then cleared her throat. 'Can't imagine that Gaia would be too happy about this,' she gestured towards Jay. 'A living person, dreaming in the realm of the dead? It's not natural. What if Gaia tries to cast her out and it ends up hurting her?'

'Them,' Jay's small voice muttered. The four ghosts turned. 'Um, I'm a them? Not a her. I'm nonbinary, I'm not a girl or a boy, I –'

'Oh, I know what that means!' Rita grinned apologetically. 'Sorry for assuming, hon. I just meant that … well, your presence here goes against everything Gaia does, which is keeping up the natural order of things. They might try to get rid of you.'

'But that might be a good thing,' Ezekiel argued, adjusting his glasses. 'If you're alive, you shouldn't be here, even in your sleep. It's probably a result of trauma, maybe something to do with your amnesia, too,'

Rita rolled her eyes and mumbled, 'God, here we go,'

Ezekiel spoke over her with a sharp glare in her direction. '*But,* if Gaia can fix this for you, it'll probably be much better for your health in the long run.'

Jay didn't look convinced. They had wrapped their arms around their middle and seemed to sink into themselves. 'I don't know …'

They looked like a lost puppy, and Olive couldn't help but feel sorry for them. She sighed impatiently. 'Look at them! They don't want to meet Gaia, they're just a scared kid! Haven't they been through enough already?'

She caught Jay smiling at her with a shy look of gratitude.

Ezekiel sighed deeply. 'What are you suggesting? That we don't tell Gaia about them?'

Olive looked him dead in the eye, lifting her chin so she was ever-so-slightly looking down at him. 'That's exactly what I'm suggesting.'

Picking up on the tension between them, Marcus exhaled in a whistle. 'We'll keep you a secret, alright? Who knows, you might wake up and never come back here again. But if you do, we'll let you decide if you want to figure this out. Sound good?'

Jay bit their lip and nodded, looking down. 'Yeah. Thanks.'

Olive opened her mouth to speak, when a sudden gust of wind picked up all the leaves surrounding them. The bugs in the area started scurrying in the same direction, back in the direction they'd come from.

'Gaia's coming,' Olive said in a whisper. 'They're just passing through, though. It's ok. They won't see you.'

She was half reassuring Jay, and half convincing herself. Even without Jay there, Olive wasn't looking forward to seeing Gaia after their last meeting. But the ghosts had witnessed this before – Gaia sometimes sent creatures to scout the forests, getting a sense of how nature was holding up in that area. Gaia themselves rarely made an appearance during these check-ups.

Out of the distant trees stepped the fox fairy. She walked forward without acknowledging the group, until she stood a few feet away. Her inky black eyes were inscrutable as she stared at them collectively. All five stood still as she watched them, and finally, her head moved the slightest bit towards Jay. A small blank smile curved up the uncannily canine face, and she walked silently in the direction that the bugs had gone.

Olive felt herself holding her breath and, taken off-guard by the unfamiliar panic in her chest, gulped down air in a gasp. She turned to say something reassuring to Jay, but as she did, she saw that Jay's form had begun to fade.

'What's happening?' They said, panicked. They held their hands up in front of their face. Olive could see their eyes through their fingers.

'It's ok, you'll be ok,' Olive said as they disappeared before her eyes.

'Can you help me? Please, I don't know where –' their pleas were cut off as they vanished entirely. In a few seconds, there was no trace of the adolescent who had stood there moments before.

Chapter Three

THE GROUP STOOD TOGETHER in silence, staring at the space where Jay had been. Rita rubbed her temples. 'Well, that was a lot to process.'

'Mmm. That all would've made a lot more sense if I hadn't had that last glass of wine.' Marcus said, picking up his guitar and putting the strap over his shoulder.

'What did *she* want?' Ezekiel said in a low voice. The fox fairy's appearance had shaken them all, and the fact that she had come alone, separate from her two friends, was even more disturbing.

Rita shuddered. 'I don't know, but it gave me the creeps. Think she's going to tell Gaia about Jay?'

Ezekiel shrugged. 'Hard to say. She and her friends always struck me as neutral parties in all this, not really allied to anyone. But ... if she *does* tell Gaia, that makes our decision for us.'

'You really want to snitch on that poor kid?' Olive said bitterly. 'We don't know what Gaia will do to them. Maybe they'll cut Jay's ties to this world, or *maybe* they'll decide that Jay belongs here, and take their soul for good.'

'You seem pretty protective of a kid you just met.' Marcus said. He kept his tone light, but Olive still heard the accusatory undertones.

'I know what they're going through.' She hugged herself just as Jay had done before. 'I know how it feels to wake up somewhere and see that everyone but you has a clue what's going on. I just think they need a little sympathy right now, not a confrontation with a creepy forest spirit.'

The truth was that Olive was happy to know someone else had the same problem. When she first arrived on this plane, the other ghosts had already been dead a long time and had gotten to know each other. If she wasn't the abnormality, if every other ghost had lost their memories as well, then she wouldn't have felt so alone. That loneliness, that feeling of always being the outsider no matter how close she got to the others – that was something that seeped through every memory she had. She wasn't sure of the extent of Jay's amnesia, but knowing they must feel similarly made her feel an instant connection to them.

Rita sighed gently. 'I get it. Can we talk about this tomorrow, though? I need to get some sleep while I'm still able to lose consciousness.'

Marcus nodded. 'I second that. Hopefully Gaia's life magic runs out before our hangovers can set in.'

Olive half-heartedly helped Marcus and Ezekiel pack up the glasses and bring them back to the house. There was still clearly some tension between Ezekiel and Olive. She knew she had reacted strongly against telling Gaia about Jay, but after Gaia's reluctance to give up any information, Olive wasn't feeling like divulging any of her own secrets. If she was being honest with herself, she liked the idea of knowing something that Gaia didn't.

Ezekiel pulled her aside before her and Rita left. 'If you're still willing to try hypnosis ... well, I can't guarantee that anything will happen, but it's better than doing nothing. I can't imagine what you're going through, but my door is always open if there's anything I can do.'

Olive wasn't too stubborn to not recognise an apology when she heard one. 'Thanks, Zeke,' she said, smiling.

By the time she and Rita had gotten to their door, Olive could definitely feel her body growing tired. Sleepiness was a pleasant feeling, tempting her to drop where she stood and give in to blissful, blank sleep. No thoughts could crowd her mind then.

The others had spoken about dreams before, but none of them had any here, even with the substitute for life that Gaia granted them. Olive didn't feel like she was being robbed of too much; it was just nice not to think about anything for a few hours.

Before she could make her way to her bed, Rita sat her down at the table. 'So, that sure was something, wasn't it?'

Olive crossed her legs, leaning back into her chair. 'Sure was. Do you think Jay will be alright? What happened to them back there?'

Rita kicked her feet up onto the table, still wearing her biker boots. 'I think they probably just woke up. They'll be fine. But I don't think it's any of our business.'

Olive pursed her lips. 'That's not fair. As far as we know, we're the only ghosts around this area. If we turn them away ... I mean, we don't really know what else is in the spirit realm! We've only ever been in Gaia's forest. What if there are other things like Gaia, but worse? We're just going to let Jay deal with that on their own?'

Rita regarded her carefully. 'You seem awfully worked up about this. That reminds me ... being so insistent on not telling Gaia? That isn't some kind of petty way to get back at them for not telling you about your memories?'

Olive tensed, her gaze turning sour. 'Of course not. I'm just worried about Jay.' she said, but her voice was quiet and bitter.

Rita tilted her head, a sad smile of sympathy on her lips. 'I'm not mad at you, ok? I just want to know what's going on with you.'

Olive huddled into herself as she felt tears prick in her eyes. 'I'm being awful, I know I am. I'm just so *tired* of waiting with no way of knowing where the finish line is.'

'Oh, Olly ...' Rita got up from her chair and walked over to Olive, wrapping her arms around her roommate. She knelt on her knees and pressed Olive's head into her shoulder, slowly rubbing her back as Olive let herself cry. 'I know, sweetie, I know. This has been so hard on you, but you're strong. We'll figure this out. You can hold on until then, right?'

Olive sobbed, finding it hard to breathe with the pain in her chest. She finally nodded, managing to whimper an 'mm hmm' into Rita's shoulder. It felt good to be held like that, to know that someone was on her side. Rita kissed her forehead lightly. Olive smiled tearfully as they locked eyes, and then she cupped Rita's face, bringing their lips together. Rita kept one hand on Olive's back and slid the other one up the back of her neck, threading her fingers through Olive's hair. The two of them were pressed together so closely that they could feel each other's heartbeats pumping as one. More tears fell from Olive's eyes and Rita moved to kiss them away, kiss each freckle on her cheeks until Olive was laughing. Eventually, Rita pulled away, stroking the side of Olive's face. She leaned close and whispered, tickling Olive's ear with her breath, 'You should get some sleep, honey.'

Olive took a shuddering breath, still recovering from her tears. She smiled up at Rita, using her shoulder to lift herself up out of the chair. 'You should too. Honey.'

She walked upstairs, feeling lightheaded and dizzy, though whether it was from the alcohol or the crying or both, she couldn't tell. She took a good look at herself in the vanity mirror. It was strange, seeing her reflection so little. Though she never changed, seeing her reflection for the first time in a while was always surprising. She never looked the way she remembered. Her hair was shorter than she thought, and limper. She could never remember if her eyes were green or brown, but looking at them now, they were clearly hazel. She had more freckles than she'd thought, a smattering all over her face as clustered as a constellation. She pressed her hands to her round cheeks, squishing her face up. Her pale skin was red and blotchy around the eyes. She didn't like the way her dried tears felt on her skin.

She clung to the memory of Rita's kisses on her skin, knowing that the sensation would disappear in the morning. She and Rita had never discussed exactly what their relationship was, but she knew it was a similar situation to Marcus and Ezekiel. Did the two really love each other, or was it just two people in a similar situation clinging to the only person they could really feel loved by? Olive wasn't sure. She didn't like to think about Rita's past girlfriend, and Rita never brought her up.

Olive went through a dozen hypothetical situations in her mind. If Gaia made good on their promise, would the ghosts keep the memories of their afterlife? Rita and

Olive had been born decades apart, regardless. Would Rita forget about her, once she had Carla back? Was Olive only a placeholder? Or would Rita keep her in her mind, reminiscing about a love that could never be? Maybe, by some miracle, they would meet in life. Rita would be four decades older, maybe unrecognisable in her old age. But Olive would know her.

Feeling like her head was full of cotton, Olive cleared the empty bottles from on top of her blanket and laid down, closing her eyes. She savoured each deep breath she took, in through the nose, out through the mouth, and before she knew it, she was in a deep, peaceful, empty sleep.

***

'So how is this supposed to work, exactly?'

It was the next morning, and Olive was lying on one of Ezekiel's couches. It wasn't a fancy one like the psychologists used in the old movies Olive had seen, just an ordinary couch. When she'd woken up that morning, she had felt a disappointing lack of sensation. Breathing had become a habit at this point, but it was no longer refreshing like it had been last night. She felt no hunger, no tiredness, no wind against her face or sun on her skin. Just the ground beneath her feet and the sense of emptiness in her stomach.

Ezekiel flicked through some books on the mahogany desk. 'It's really just a kind of trance. I guide you through it, and you relax enough to let me plant ideas in your head. Just ... helping you find the memories, if we can.'

Olive raised an eyebrow. 'You never actually got your degree, did you?'

Ezekiel sharply shut the book he was reading and gave her an incredulous look. 'No, I didn't. Thanks for rubbing it in.'

Olive smirked, making herself comfortable. 'So, what, do I have to close my eyes or something?'

'If you want. The important thing here is to be open to it. Of course, if you're uncomfortable with any part of this, we'll stop but ... just keep an open mind, ok?'

'Hmm. Ok.' Olive closed her eyes and leaned her head back on the couch. 'Fire away, then.'

Ezekiel took a deep breath. Olive heard him taking a seat at his desk chair, shuffling pages. 'Huh ... most of this technique is reliant on breath control, so ... just pretend that you actually need to breathe, alright?'

Olive snickered, still with her eyes closed. 'Nervous?'

'A little,' she could hear the smile in his voice, and she felt relieved. He couldn't have been too annoyed with her.

'Now, I want you to imagine that you're in your house. You're on the first floor, and as you walk towards the back of the house, you notice a door that you haven't seen before. You open it, and on the other side is a dark staircase leading down. Do you see it?'

She felt ridiculous, but she went along with it, forming the images in her mind. She thought the pictures were just supposed to come to her as he spoke, but his words sounded stilted and she felt like she was forcing herself to follow his instructions. She tried not to sound too bored. 'Yeah, I see it.'

'There aren't any lights, so you have to hold onto the railing as you walk down, carefully feeling for each step. As you go further down the staircase, you see a faint light coming from below. You reach the bottom, and there's an empty room lit up by a single light bulb hanging from the ceiling. In the middle of the room is a box. What the box looks like is up to you. It can be a shoebox if you want. Maybe it's more like a music box, with a latch.'

Olive laughed in her mind. She still didn't feel close to being in a trance, but she felt obliged to humour him anyway. She pictured a dark wooden box with a golden latch, standing on four golden legs.

'Whatever it is, it isn't locked. I want you to imagine that this box is the darkest part of your mind, the part that's most obscured by shadows. The information is there, you just need to reach it. You don't have to force it open, just let it come to you naturally. I want you to open the box now. Really focus on the inside of it.'

He stopped talking, and Olive guessed she was meant to be imagining the contents of this mysterious box. She felt like there was supposed to be some huge revelation, a grand vision that was meant to reveal itself to her.

'Tell me what you see,'

Olive exhaled for a long time. 'Nothing.' She opened her eyes. She could see the disappointment in his eyes, even though he was trying to hide it. 'I'm sorry, Ezekiel.'

He sighed, re-adjusting his papers without looking at her. 'Don't be sorry. I don't know what I expected. I haven't practised this before; I didn't really know what I was doing ...'

'It's not you, Zeke, it's me.' Olive sat up, swinging her legs off of the side of her couch. 'Rita was right, this was never going to work on me. Thanks for trying, though.'

Ezekiel leaned against his desk defeatedly. 'I really wish I could do more to help, Olive.'

She stood and placed a hand on his forearm. 'It's ok. You tried. I really appreciate it, you know.'

He smiled sadly. 'What are friends for, right? We're all here together. I'd feel pretty selfish if I didn't try to help.'

Olive laughed. 'You, my friend, are far from selfish.'

He walked her to the door and they passed Marcus in the dining room. He looked curious, but he could probably guess from their expressions that the experiment hadn't gone as planned. Olive felt more disappointed than she was expecting to. She knew from the start that it wasn't going to work but that didn't mean she hadn't been hopeful. It wasn't the hypnotism in particular that gave her hope, but just the idea that it *might* work, or even open the gates for something else to start working in her mind. Maybe it was like Ezekiel had said, and the hypnosis had failed because her heart just wasn't in it. But maybe it was something else, like Rita had suggested.

If Gaia or some kind of higher power was purposefully blocking her memories … she couldn't imagine what she had done in her life that would warrant that. Was it possible that her memory loss was a punishment for something she'd done in life? It didn't seem likely. As far as Olive could tell, the spirit realm wasn't concerned with punishing *or* rewarding its inhabitants. Still, it was the only explanation she could think of that made any sense.

Olive waved goodbye to Marcus and Ezekiel, but instead of going straight home, she decided to take a walk around the forest. She knew she'd eventually find her way back home. She just needed a chance to clear her head a bit, recover from her uneventful hypnotism session. And if she was being honest with herself, she was kind of hoping she would see Jay. She wondered if Gaia's presence had forced them to leave somehow. And what exactly had the fox fairy been doing there, without the other two in tow? It was bothering Olive more than it should have. There was just something so off-putting about that girl, the way she stood unnaturally still, like she was setting prey. And the smile she gave after seeing Jay was enough to chill Olive's cold, dead heart. It also made her question how much she really knew about the spirit realm. Rita, Marcus and Ezekiel were the only other ghosts Olive had met, but that didn't mean there weren't others like them. And what happened to the ghosts that Gaia didn't manage to catch? Were they able to move on from the spiritual realm, or were they stuck here forever?

By this point, Olive had passed her usual part of the forest. The trees were thicker here, clustering together and blotting out most of the sunlight. A small shadow flitted past, too quickly for Olive to register what it was. The wind blew hard, and even though it didn't have any effect on Olive, she could tell it was heavier than it had been just minutes ago. More and more shadows started darting past her and they hit her body heavily. Olive jumped back in shock. She had begun to think that they were just little birds, but real birds should not have been able to touch her. They were flying towards her in a swarm, whacking her and then continuing on, flying further into the darkness of the forest. Not used to the unfamiliar pain, Olive tried to avoid them, running to shelter herself behind a tree, but they kept coming at her. She realised that the sound they were making was not merely the fluttering of wings, but whispers. Harsh, crackling whispers so cacophonous that Olive could not tell them apart, let alone decipher what they were saying. These things that could somehow *touch* her – they were definitely dangerous. But Olive's curiosity got the better of her. It seemed like the only way she was getting out of there was to move *with* the swarm, rather than against it. She was already dead; what was the worst that could happen?

The shapes slowed their pace as soon as she decided to follow them, and they seemed to fly around her instead of into her. As she went on, the trees around her started shifting from tall oaks with orange leaves, to darker, heavier looking trees. The forest floor lost its layer of leaves and grass, and the dirt beneath became marshy. The plants progressively turned greener, the trees reaching taller and spreading wider, fanned leaves, their bark becoming smooth. Moss slowly crept up every surface, covering the ground so that when Olive placed her foot down in front of her, she found herself stepping through a few inches of water. The fluttering shapes around her stopped and disappeared. She looked up. This was a swamp, and it was far from Gaia's domain.

Chapter Four

Olive turned around slowly, trying to get a grip on her surroundings, but there was nothing there that she recognised. The sun wasn't visible under the thick foliage of the trees, but it was dark enough to be night, even though it had been morning when she had left Gaia's forest.

The same whispers that had come from the flying shapes echoed again, but this time quiet, muffled. Olive looked to find the source of the sound, but she couldn't see any more shadows speeding past. And then she looked down, into the water that she was standing in.

The moss, or algae, obscured most of the surface of the water, but there were just enough gaps for Olive to see dark silhouettes flicker across it. She stepped back with a gasp, and then took a few more steps backwards until she was no longer standing in water. She saw with horror a few shadows clinging to her foot, which slipped back into the water. The whispers grew louder, and it was clear they were definitely human voices, though she still couldn't distinguish any individual words.

Something bubbled beneath the surface. The whispers grew in volume and came together as a unified screech as Olive watched a dark shape, like a splotch of ink, appear in the middle of the swamp and spread over the water. Olive covered her ears, but it did nothing to stifle the noise. Something deep inside of her was screaming at her to run before the thing could surface, but she felt rooted to the spot.

A slick mess of algae-covered vines and sticks was the first thing to come out of the water. The algae on the surface melded into this new shape, clinging to it as it slowly rose up. From behind the veil of aquatic greenery came two round, pale yellow eyes with thin pupils. Olive was standing too far away to see any real details, but even from a distance, the eyes were decidedly reptilian.

The shape rose higher, revealing a face that was humanoid in the vaguest of terms. There was a nose, and lips pulled back into a flat, crocodilian smile, but the face itself did not appear to be made of skin and flesh. It was dotted with algae and rot, and was a dark teal colour, slick as the skin of a frog. A neck revealed itself, moss and algae clinging to the tops of shoulders and sticking to the form as it continued to rise, like a makeshift dress obscuring the figure that continued to rise taller, almost reaching the tops of the trees. Two long, dangling arms swung at its sides, ending in hooked fingers with webbing between them. Olive watched in horror, her mind screaming louder but her legs refused to move.

The thing in the swamp towered high above her, then looked down and caught her in the grip of its cold eyes. The smile widened, the lips cracked and almost scaly. From between them Olive could see tightly packed teeth, dark yellow with rot.

'You're just in time,' the thing croaked. Its thin voice hissed like a snake, melodious in a way, but whispery and seeming to echo throughout the swamp.

Olive gazed up at the thing, frozen in place. Her voice wavered when she spoke, and it came out so quietly she wasn't sure if it could be heard, let alone if she had actually said it out loud. 'Who ... who are you?'

The thing sank down as it laughed a terrible chuckle, its shoulders shaking as it sunk down to just above Olive's eye level. It blinked once. A thin, transparent film slid across its eyes before its crusty, scaly lids closed and opened, the left one just a beat slower than the right. 'You don't know me, do you? Never mind. You're here now, and that is what's important.'

Olive couldn't look at the thing's eyes for more than a second without revulsion. She fixed her eyes on a tree on the other side of the swamp and tried to strengthen her resolve. 'You didn't answer my question. Who are you? Why am I here? What do you want from me?'

The thing chuckled again. 'Smart girl. It's good to ask questions. Good to demand answers. That *is* what you want, isn't it? Answers?'

Olive narrowed her eyes and fumbled to come up with a good response, but the creature cut her off with a dismissive wave of its webbed hand. 'But I'm getting ahead of myself. I will answer your question. My name was Hazel, once ... ah, but no one has called me by that name in many years. But that's not what you want to know, is it?

You want to know *what* I am, you're just too polite to ask it in those terms.'

Olive was feeling less and less like being polite as the conversation continued, but she didn't need to speak. Hazel seemed satisfied with carrying the conversation alone. 'I was like you, once. I was alive. And then I was dead. I was taken in by the forest spirit, as you were, and bound to serve them. They gave you a similar contract, did they not? Collect these ... *trinkets* for them on the fragile promise that they would give you your life back?'

Olive didn't have to nod. Her face betrayed her, frowning, and Hazel smirked. 'I played their game for a long time, but I grew bored of that. See, I knew they would never give me what I really wanted. But it was torture to wait around in this empty space, feeling nothing, *being* nothing. I wanted more. I figured out a way to feel *alive* without paying off a debt with no foreseeable end.' She turned to Olive with a knowing smile. 'I could show you. You're just the same as I was. Tired. Desperate. Searching for a purpose. But I became stronger. I became more than I had ever been in life. And I could help you do the same.'

Olive felt a chill run up her spine. 'And why would you do that?'

'Oh, it wouldn't come for free, of course,' Hazel continued. 'I have no intention of keeping you waiting here for eternity like that spirit, but I would ask a simple favour from you, if you're willing.'

There was something both mischievous and dangerous in her eyes. Any kind of favour this ... demon, or whatever Hazel was, wanted could only be bad news.

Seeing her hesitation, Hazel spoke up. 'You're not convinced, are you? I'm offering you a good deal here. I can teach you how to feel alive for more than just one night. I can teach you to become part of the world around you, to feel the energy and power of everything you come into contact with.'

She suddenly leant towards Olive, her arms pulling her across the surface of the water with lightning speed until her face was looming over Olive's. 'But that's not enough for you, is it? You want more.' Her lips split up in a wicked grin. 'You want your memories back.'

Olive finally found her feet, stepping back and planting her feet. She looked straight into Hazel's eyes, trying her hardest not to blink or waver. 'What do you know about my memories?'

Hazel watched her coldly, a thick white tongue poking through her teeth to lick her lips maliciously. A deep rumble emanated from her body in a mockery of laughter. 'Oh, I know a lot about you, *Olive*. And I can tell you exactly who you are, if you agree to do something for me in exchange.'

Olive chewed her lip. She should not be here. She should have run as soon as she noticed anything out of the ordinary. But she hadn't. She had stayed, and now that she'd heard *something* about her memories, she couldn't turn her back on them. She was caught now. It would be trading one otherworldly pact for another, but at least this one promised answers. 'What exactly would I be doing for you?'

The scenery flickered around them for a moment, and even Hazel seemed startled. The dark swamp flashed back to the golden autumnal forest of Gaia's domain and back. Hazel tilted her head, letting out a few audible cracks from her neck, and clicked her tongue. 'Time is running short, my dear. Just think on the idea for now, and come back when you're ready. I will find you.'

She smiled cruelly on the last sentence, and more of the dark shadows began to rise from the water, swirling around her form. As Olive panicked and tried to run, her vision flicked back and forth between the swamp and the forest in a dizzying array of colour and light. It finally settled on the forest, and Olive was left standing in front of the lake, alone.

***

She took a while to compose herself. The wind was blowing gently around the forest, indicating Gaia's presence. Olive stared at the surface of the lake, half expecting something dark and shadowy to emerge from it, but not even a reflection greeted her.

She knew Hazel was nothing but trouble, and that staying away was the safest option. But she had *been* safe for decades. No matter what she tried to tell herself, she was intrigued by Hazel's proposal. Olive was not interested in becoming some sort of amphibious swamp demon, but she was curious about how Hazel went from being a ghost like her to the spiritual being that stood before her moments ago. She was also curious about the extent of Hazel's power. She had mentioned feeling alive for longer than Gaia would allow. *That* was something that spoke to Olive. Unlike the other ghosts, the brief hours where she felt true sensation were the only taste she had ever had of being a real human. The false life that Gaia gifted was sweet, but it was barely enough to satisfy Olive before it disappeared, leaving her an empty shell. If she could feel like that for a full day, a week, a month ... the idea alone was enough to tempt her.

And then there were her memories. How could Hazel know about that? Though she clearly had some elemental powers, Hazel was not the same as Gaia. She couldn't just *know*, unless something about Olive so blatantly screamed post-mortem amnesia. If Hazel knew about her memories, surely she must know something about why they went missing? Maybe she could even restore them. She clearly had *something* she was willing to share, for a price. If there was a chance to learn anything about her past, wasn't it worth it to at least try? Maybe she would go back, and just ask what it was that Hazel wanted so badly. It didn't seem like she had a choice, since Hazel was able to find her so easily the first time.

Breathing a heavy, completely useless sigh, Olive took the long way back to the house, passing the farm on the way. She was still mulling over whether to tell the others about Hazel, but she already knew what they would say. They would stop her from going back, get her to tell Gaia, and make her lose any chance of discovering more about herself. She did feel a twinge of guilt at the thought of not telling Rita. It would be hard to keep secrets from her, but Olive needed to get her head around the issue and decide what to do next on her own.

She trailed her fingers over the wooden fence posts of the paddock, and a small flock of sheep stared at her with their eery horizontal pupils. A couple of the older ewes stepped forward, as if challenging her to come closer. Olive enjoyed hanging around the farm. Animals could see ghosts, and while it was fair to assume that they got the sense that ghosts were different to regular people, that didn't stop some of them from looking for treats. The farm's dog, a raggedy black and white collie chained up outside his doghouse, started barking at Olive. She watched him with some amusement, feeling a little bad that she couldn't go and pet him. The door to the farmhouse opened and the farmer emerged from his morning tea break, looking around wildly for any sign of an intruder or a stray animal coming for his flock, but seeing nothing, he grumbled something about the 'stupid mutt' and went back inside.

Olive smiled to herself. Sometimes it was nice not to be seen.

By the time she made it back to the house, it was well past midday. She could see Rita crouched on the ground amongst the leaves, leaning her back against the wall. She was picking up leaves and setting them alight with her hands, extinguishing the flames before the leaf burnt up completely. Every now and then she would breathe in the smoke, and breathe it back out again in a different vibrant colour.

Each of the ghosts had received some form of elemental powers when they made their deal with Gaia. They had a small amount of influence in the physical realm, but for the most part, they were just for show. They each had an affinity for a certain part of nature; Ezekiel could control the air, Marcus could manipulate water to his will, and Olive had a knack for making plants grow, like she had made the thorns wind around her hand at the picnic last night. Rita's affinity was with fire, a talent which she pinned on her 'going out in a blaze of glory'. Olive wasn't exactly sure if these powers corresponded with their deaths, but it was something she had theorised with before, when she would try to guess how she died. It made sense, considering that Marcus had drowned, and Ezekiel had fallen from a great height.

Rita looked up as Olive approached, then vanished the flame from her hand with a small smile. She stood up without touching her hands to the ground, and crossed the distance between the two in a few easy steps. She tilted her head with a calculating frown, looking Olive up and down. 'Where have you been all day? Ezekiel came over a while ago, he said you'd finished hours ago.'

Olive shrugged, letting her hair fall in front of her face. 'It didn't go well at all. Nothing happened. Can't say I'm surprised.' She shifted her weight from one foot to the other. 'I just went for a walk. I needed to clear my head. I guess the fact that it failed had more of an effect on me than I thought it would.'

Rita's expression softened to one of pity, and she held out her hand for Olive to take. Their fingers linking up, she swung both of their hands together. 'That's ok, honey. At least you tried, right?'

Olive hummed contentedly and smiled. 'Yeah, I guess so,'

Rita gazed adoringly at her for a few seconds, then released her hand. She stared over Olive's shoulder. 'It's my anniversary tomorrow.'

Olive blinked. 'Oh,'

It didn't seem like it had been a year since the last time they had celebrated Rita's death. Or maybe Olive just hadn't thought about it since she didn't have an anniversary of her own. While she couldn't exactly relate, she understood that there were a lot of emotions associated with the day of a person's death. A lot of mixed feelings, longing, pretending not to be upset when it was obvious how close to tears they really were. The four of them usually gathered together, listening to the person's favourite music and dancing. If the anniversary happened to coincide with the procuring of one of Gaia's tokens, they would go out and buy a birthday cake, splurging on drinks and snacks.

The other three spent the day reminiscing about their lives, their families, the people they loved, and Olive never knew what to say. She tried not to be bitter, but it was hard to listen and not be able to contribute anything. They would notice how uncomfortable she looked and try to persuade her to have another drink, or put on another movie, but she would shrug them off and tell them to go back to enjoying themselves. She hated herself for being jealous, but the feeling was there. She couldn't do anything about it.

'I want to show you something tomorrow,' Rita said, interrupting Olive's train of thought. 'I know thinking about your memory has been getting you down lately. And I *know* that I can't fix everything for you, but there's something I want you to see. You might never understand why I want to stay here, but maybe this will help give it context.'

Olive frowned and tilted her head. 'What do you mean? What are you going to show me?'

Rita raised an eyebrow and tapped Olive on the nose playfully. 'You'll just have to wait and see.'

Chapter Five

Olive and Rita tried to fill in the afternoon around the house, but Olive's racing mind wouldn't let her rest. The girls quickly grew tired of re-reading old books and sketching the trees from the window, so they made their way back into the forest where they had seen Jay last night. Olive picked up a branch larger than she was from the ground and swung it around as she skipped with listless energy. Rita watched her and laughed, little wisps of blue smoke puffing out of her mouth, then she gave a small wave and yelled out. Olive looked up and saw Marcus and Ezekiel walking towards them, and she waved her branch high in the air.

'Careful with that,' Marcus said, laughing. 'What's going on?'

'We're waiting for Jay,' Olive dropped the branch on the ground and stepped on it with one foot, pulling it up with her hands until it broke in two. 'We were hoping they'd come back tonight, unless Gaia chased them off or something.'

'We had the same thought,' Ezekiel said, sitting and leaning against a tree. 'If they don't show up, it's probably safe to assume that their visit here was just a one-off thing. If they do come back ... well, I guess we're back to where we started.'

Olive wielded one half of her broken branch like a spear and pointed it at him from a safe distance. 'And you're not going to snitch on them to Gaia?'

Ezekiel batted the stick away with a roll of his eyes and an exasperated smirk. 'I promise I won't. Jay looked terrified enough as it was with just us – they don't need to deal with Gaia just yet.'

Marcus ruffled his hair affectionately. 'See? He does have a heart.'

Olive got comfortable, tucking her legs up underneath her. She willed a few small white flowers to pop up from the ground next to her, lightly brushing her fingers over their soft petals. Staring out into the distance, she listened for any sound and looked for any shape that could have been Jay.

She also kept an eye out for any of the dark shapes that had led her to Hazel, but nothing seemed amiss. Still, she felt on edge, waiting for some kind of trap to be sprung.

The heads of the four ghosts turned when they heard branches snapping underfoot. Jay stepped out of the same place they had appeared last night, wearing a red hoodie and a bashful smile. They waved nervously, one hand behind their back. 'Hey, guys ...'

Olive grinned and leapt up to greet them. She was tempted to give them a hug, but she thought better of it when she noticed how nervous they still looked. 'Hi Jay! It's good to see you again. How are you?'

'We didn't know if we'd see you again,' Rita said.

Jay laughed awkwardly, adjusting their beanie. 'Yeah, I wasn't sure either. It kind of freaked me out last night, but I woke up in the hospital again and I guess I thought I was just dreaming. But I'm here now! So, yeah. Guess I still have no clue what's going on.'

'Well, we're glad to have you here,' Ezekiel said in his sympathetic therapist voice. 'We were getting a bit worried about you.'

'You ... you didn't tell that spirit thing about me, did you?' They asked, jiggling their foot so that their heel tapped against the ground in a frantic pattern.

Olive, Rita and Marcus all turned to look at Ezekiel, who wilted under their collective gaze and sighed. He rolled his eyes at his friends, but his voice was kind when he spoke to Jay. 'No, and we're not going to either, unless you tell us you're ok with it.'

Jay breathed a sigh of relief, laughing softly. 'That's cool, thanks so much. I um, I was getting pretty worked up about that.' They looked at the group in front of them, and then started absently picking at the bark of a tree beside them. 'I don't think I got your names last time? Sorry, I meant to ask ...'

Rita chuckled. 'Don't worry about it, you had plenty of other things to worry about. I'm Rita, this is Olive,' she gave Olive's shoulder a squeeze. 'The tall one is Marcus, and Glasses over there is Ezekiel.'

She held out her hand for Jay to shake. Jay reached out with a delighted smile, but their hand passed straight through Rita's. Their expression turned to one of comical shock, and then Rita pulled her hand away with a mischievous grin. 'Gotcha,'

It took Jay a second, but they started laughing, matching Rita's energy. 'That's a pretty cool trick,' They seemed to be loosening up a bit, gaining confidence. 'So … what's it like being a ghost? What kind of stuff can you guys do?'

Olive looked behind her at the small patch of grass they had been seated at before. 'Why don't you come and sit with us? We can show you a few things.'

Jay followed her gaze. 'Oh … I mean, if that's ok with you? I don't want to intrude or anything.'

'Are you kidding?' Marcus said, grinning. 'You showing up is the most interesting thing that's happened here in decades!'

Jay looked very young in that moment, almost bursting with nervousness and excitement. 'Well, if you're sure …'

Olive led them back to the spot on the grass. The five of them spread out amongst the trees, Rita and Olive making green grass grow to soften the ground for Jay. Rita, Ezekiel and Marcus started talking about their lives, telling stories about the people they knew and the decades they grew up in, and how things had changed since then. Olive tuned most of it out, having heard it before, but then Jay's gaze fell expectantly on her and she snapped out of it.

She straightened up, feeling everyone else's eyes on her as well, and her sense of being the odd one out strengthened. She tried to lighten the mood with a light laugh. 'I'm a bit of a special case, actually. I'm kind of in the same situation as you.'

Jay tilted their head, taking time to register what she meant. 'You have amnesia too? How does that work with ghosts?'

Olive shrugged, grinning. 'I have no idea! I wish I knew.'

Jay nodded, an appreciative smile on their face. 'I know how you feel. Not about the ghost stuff, I mean. The amnesia. It's ... nice to know someone else knows what it feels like.'

Olive returned the smile. 'Well you know, if you ever want to talk about our shared experiences ...'

She glanced at Ezekiel and then an idea struck her. 'Oh, hey! Zeke and I just tried a bit of a hypnosis session. It didn't do much for me, but maybe it could work for you?'

Ezekiel watched them, waiting eagerly for a chance to speak, but Jay withdrew. 'Nah, I don't think so. I've tried it with a couple of therapists, nothing really happened.

I don't know if there's anything that will fix it, actually. Everyone keeps telling me to wait it out, but I'm not so sure.'

They sighed, running their fingers through the grass at their feet. 'People keep showing up in my hospital room. They have photos of us, or they talk about things we did together, but I have no clue who they are. It feels like they're talking about someone else, like I woke up in the wrong body and everyone thinks I'm a different person.'

They ripped out a few blades in frustration. 'I hate the way they look when they realise I don't know them. It's like they blame me for this, like I'm just not trying hard enough. Sometimes I feel like I have to pretend, just to spare *their* feelings.'

Olive desperately wished she could give them some kind of comfort, but she couldn't even touch their hand or pull them into a hug. 'That isn't fair on you, though. You've got enough to worry about as it is.'

'I know, but ... it just feels like everybody is waiting for me to get over this so that things can go back to normal. I'm waiting too, but I have no idea what 'normal' is! I keep hoping that everything will make sense eventually, but right now I just feel lost.'

They had said all the things Olive felt but had never put into words. Her heart ached for them, but at the same time she felt justified in her feelings. It wasn't just her being a brat about her memories. She wanted to say *See? Someone else feels the way I do*, but she didn't want to seem like she was taking joy from Jay's pain.

'I'm sorry, you don't want to hear about my problems.' Jay said, shaking their head with an awkward laugh. 'I can't say this in front of anyone else. I don't want them to feel bad, or that they're upsetting me. It's just nice to talk to someone who isn't expecting a miracle from me.'

Rita nodded thoughtfully, her eyes quickly shooting over to Olive. 'You're not under any pressure here to remember. We're not going to push you.'

'You've done everything you can to get your memories back, haven't you? If there was anything more that you could do, you'd do it.' Olive was trying to sound sympathetic, but she was searching, digging for more gratification. She wanted to know that Jay would make the same choice she had, if they were given the option. Wouldn't they?

Jay just shrugged. 'I guess so. I don't really have the energy to care about that right now, though. It's exhausting. trying to remember. I just want to be able to exist as I am now, you know?'

Olive didn't know. She wanted more than anything to regain her memories, and she'd never even known what she was missing. How could Jay have something to long for, and *not* want to return to it?

'But ... but how can you be ok with not knowing who you are? Don't you want to feel whole again?'

Rita put her hand on Olive's shoulder, applying a little more tension than was necessary. 'Easy, Ol. This isn't about you.'

Olive paused and saw that everyone was staring at her. She'd let herself get carried away. Again. She dropped her gaze and gave Jay a bashful smile.

'I'm sorry,' she said, trying to save face. 'Of course, that's your call to make. I'm just ... projecting, I guess.'

She was granted a forgiving look from Jay, who shrugged and nodded. 'I get it. I gotta admit, it was scary to wake up and realise I'd missed the last ten years of my life. I can't imagine what it'd be like to not remember anything.'

'It's not so bad here,' Olive said nonchalantly, though in the moment she wanted to be anywhere else. 'There's a lot of cool stuff I can do that I wouldn't have been able to do when I was alive.'

Jay tilted their head. 'Oh yeah? Like what?'

Olive grinned. 'So many things. It's like magic.'

The four of them told Jay about the afterlife, dispelling their misconceptions and answering their many questions. They talked a little bit about themselves, and the decades they lived in. Olive kept things vague, not giving away anything about her missing memories just in case Jay asked something she herself did not know the answer to. The ghosts showed Jay a little bit of the magic they all possessed, producing flowers, miniature tornadoes, tiny storm clouds and embers falling from the sky.

'That's pretty cool, how you're all from different times,' they said, then frowned in thought, staring intently at a large iris that Olive had made bloom in their hands. 'Does that mean you don't know what the internet is?'

The ghosts laughed, and Jay blushed. Rita lowered herself until she was lying down, her arms crossed underneath her head. 'Nah, we know what that is, we're not totally out of touch. We know what's going on. We buy the paper every week.'

Now it was Jay's turn to laugh. 'You guys are still reading newspapers? Wow, you really are from the past. You know if you have a phone, you can learn about everything that's going on around the world?'

'We *do* have phones, actually!' Marcus piped up. 'Picked up some older models on sale a few years ago. Don't think we ever really figured them out, though.'

'How does that work?' Jay asked with raised eyebrows. 'You pass through people when you touch them, but you can hold a phone?'

Ezekiel adjusted his glasses. 'We can choose to become corporeal when we're looking for tokens. It's not the same as being alive, and people get a weird chill if we touch them, but at least we can interact with the world.'

Jay nodded thoughtfully, chewing their lip. 'So if you're a ghost, do you still need to be wearing glasses?'

Marcus snickered, running his fingers over Ezekiel's hand. 'Nah, he just wears his because they look cute.'

'How about you tell us about yourself?' Ezekiel said, giving him a gentle shove. 'We've talked about ourselves enough, I think.'

Jay shared a grin with Olive, then looked away bashfully. 'Uh, sure! There's not much to tell. You already know how

I ended up in hospital, because uh, because I almost died. So let's see, um …'

They bit their lip, tilting their head in thought. 'I live with my mum and my older brother – my parents are divorced – and we have a couple of cats. My life is pretty boring, I guess. I play video games, I read comics, I like skateboarding … that's about it, I think? I go camping with my brother sometimes, that's fun. Levi's kind of over it now, but he comes along if mum tells him to.'

They looked down, their face growing solemn. 'I guess he probably won't be too keen on coming next time. He … he was pretty shaken up by the whole thing, the um. The near-death experience.'

Olive frowned in sympathy. 'He was there with you, wasn't he?'

Jay nodded. 'Yeah, he was. I think he blames himself for the accident, which is *stupid,* because obviously he can't control the weather.'

Rita clicked her tongue. 'Mm. That's a pretty common train of thought, in those situations. Seems like he really cares about you, though.'

Jay smiled sadly, curling their knees up towards their chest and rocking slightly. 'Yeah, I know he does.'

They stared at their shoes for a while, then put on a smile. 'You should show me your phones next time I'm here, maybe I can teach you how to use 'em properly.'

Olive smiled softly and nodded. 'We'd like that,'

She watched as Jay started fading away, just as they had last night. They stared at their hands, considerably less surprised than they were before. They looked around at the ghosts and waved their hand with the smallest turn of their wrist. 'Thanks for letting me hang out. Hopefully I'll see you guys tomorrow night?'

The ghosts nodded and waved back at them as they disappeared from view, and the forest suddenly felt colder and less vibrant.

'They're a good kid,' Marcus said after a few seconds of silence. 'Reminds me of my little brother.'

Rita nodded pensively, but Olive didn't say anything.

'Do you really think we'll be able to keep them from Gaia?' Ezekiel said quietly, almost as if he was afraid the spirit would hear him. 'I mean, even if we never tell them, surely they would have *some* way of knowing something's going on.'

Rita rolled her neck, thinking. 'That's true. But don't you think they would have found out by now anyway?

Maybe they just don't care. It's not like Jay is hurting anything.'

Olive crossed her arms around her middle. 'Look, I don't know why we would even *need* to tell Gaia in the first place. We don't owe them anything except their stupid tokens. It wasn't part of the deal to tell them about every little thing that might be out of the ordinary.'

Marcus smirked at her, and she glared back at him. 'What? I'm not trying to be petty, I'm just saying! We're not obliged to tell them anything.'

Marcus held up his hands in surrender, but he was smiling, infuriatingly. 'No, no, I agree with you! You're just being kind of ...'

'*What?*' Olive snapped. 'Spit it out, what am I being? What's so funny to you?'

Rita and Ezekiel exchanged a glance. Rita opened her mouth to interrupt them, but Marcus started speaking before she had the chance.

'You're just being a little testy, that's all,' his calm tone of voice was only frustrating Olive further. 'You've been really dead-set on hiding things from Gaia lately. It's like you're trying to rebel or something, it's ... you're kind of wasting your energy, you know?'

Olive felt thorns growing around her, pricking her skin. 'It's so easy for you to just sit back and do what they tell you, isn't it? You can go along with their deal because you know *exactly* what you're getting out of it.' She felt her temper flaring, but she had gotten a taste for anger now and she was not about to let it go. 'Bet you can't wait to get back your brother, right? Back to your family who loves you? Lucky you!'

Marcus's smile dropped, and his eyes narrowed. Olive could see that she had hurt him, but she found she was oddly satisfied with the response she had gotten.

'You think you know everything, don't know? You really think I told you everything about my life? You think I didn't hide the bad parts because they were too hard to talk about?'

'Marcus ...' Ezekiel's voice was barely audible as he tried to calm him down.

'No, she needs to hear this,' Marcus said, staring down Olive. 'It's like you think that our lives were perfect just because we can remember them. But you know what? Sometimes I wish I couldn't! I love my brother, but my life was *far* from fucking perfect, alright? If you think our lives were all good times and happy families, that's because we've only told you the things we want to remember.'

Olive dropped her gaze. She wanted to hold onto her anger, but guilt was starting to creep into her chest, and she didn't like the direction this conversation was heading in.

'You want to know how I really died? I drowned myself. It wasn't some freak tidal wave, or a boating accident, or ...' he trailed off, his voice choking as tears welled in his eyes, which he tried to wipe away before they could fall. 'I just walked into the ocean and never came out. I did it because my life sucked so much that I felt like I didn't have another option. I couldn't be who I was, I couldn't walk down the street without being treated like a criminal. I couldn't *love* who I wanted to. And the fact that you think I'm just *dying* to get back there ... it sucks, it really does, Olive.'

Her anger had wilted away completely, leaving only sadness and regret. 'Marcus, I ...'

He shook his head, wiping his eyes with his arm and turning away from her, keeping his head low. 'I'm going home.'

He took off, storm clouds gathering in the sky above, and Ezekiel ran after him after shooting a quick, conflicted glance back at Olive.

She shrunk into herself, staring at her feet in shame. 'I shouldn't have said that,'

Rita sighed heavily, finally standing up. 'No. You shouldn't have.'

Her stony silence was enough to break Olive's heart. She thought Rita was going to walk off and leave her alone, but she didn't. She looked into Olive's face with intense disappointment. 'Marcus was right, though. I think you did need to hear that. Do you get it now? How this isn't easy for us, just because we remember? Do you see why the thought of staying here is a little more comforting than going back?'

Olive nodded, covering her mouth with her hand. 'I'm sorry,'

Rita laughed through her nose, a bitter exhalation of breath. 'Don't say it to me. Say it to Marcus. But give him some space first, ok?'

Olive swallowed hard, looking up at the sky where a couple of drops of rain were beginning to fall. 'Do you think he'll forgive me?' she choked out in a small gasp.

A slight smile made its way onto Rita's face and she put a hand on Olive's shoulder. 'I'm sure he will, eventually. You'll have eternity to work it out.'

It was obvious she was trying to lighten the mood, but the words came out bitter and sharp, and Olive didn't feel like laughing.

Rita gave her shoulder a squeeze. 'C'mon, let's go home.'

Chapter Six

THE NIGHT PASSED IN near silence, with the pit of guilt growing deeper in Olive's chest with every hour gone by. What Marcus said had shaken her, and she was forced to acknowledge the bubble of naivety she had placed herself in. He was right. She had assumed they all had it better than she did. She didn't even think that the way they painted their lives to her might not have been the whole truth. She felt selfish for never thinking to pry deeper, or at least imagining how hard it must have been for the three of them, who would still be marginalised in this decade. Not to mention the discrimination they must have faced in their own times.

Knowing the truth about Marcus's death changed the way she thought of him. All his jokes, his upbeat attitude, his music ... it was all hiding so much sadness that she had not been aware of. It made her question how well she really knew these people, and she was faced with the conclusion that she only knew what they wanted her to.

When the morning finally rolled around, Olive had made sure that she rose with the sun. She went outside before she heard Rita stir, and went to work making a small garden grow around the house. Through her years in the afterlife she had discovered that she could make plants grow out of season, so she went about picturing every colourful, tropical flower that came to her mind. She made the tree in front of the house grow cherries. She conjured up a dozen vibrant, flame red tulips and gathered them up into a bouquet along with some of the tiny white flowers that Rita loved to braid into Olive's hair. She entered the house, and was glad to find Rita reading a magazine at the table, her back to the door.

Olive wrapped her arms around Rita from behind, holding the flowers in front of her face. 'Happy anniversary, babe,'

Rita smiled, but it didn't reach her eyes. She took the bouquet from Olive's hands, admiring it with an approving nod. 'This must have taken a bit of work, huh?'

'Do you like them?' Olive said, a little disappointed by her lack of obvious excitement.

Rita took one of Olive's hands, rested it on her collarbone, and pressed a kiss to it. 'They're beautiful. I love them.'

Seeing that Olive still wasn't convinced, she stood up, holding the bouquet, and walked into the kitchen, pulling open the cabinets. 'We've got to have a vase around here somewhere, right? Or a jam jar. Those are back in fashion, I think.'

Olive hopped over to join her, and went to a cabinet against the back wall. 'There's a vase in here,' she pointed up to the top shelf, which was far too high for her to reach. Just like Olive knew she would, Rita walked up behind her and raised her arm over the auburn head, retrieving the glass vase with little effort. She lowered it and walked to the sink, aiming a wry smile at Olive, and started filling the vase with water.

'There,' she said, placing the glass on the table and putting the bouquet inside it. 'Hey, thanks for this, Olly. I appreciate it, I really do.'

Olive shrugged coyly, but she couldn't help a little smile.

Rita sighed, staring at the bright red flowers. 'I was going to show you something today, wasn't I? Oh yeah, that's right.' She turned to Olive, her face suddenly serious. 'Do you know where I go every year? On this day?'

Olive blinked. 'The cemetery. Your grave.'

Rita nodded sagely with her eyes closed. 'Yep, you got it. Do you know *why* I go there?'

Olive frowned. She didn't like guessing games.

Rita's annual visits confused Olive. It seemed like doing that would only make her sad. They usually spent most of their death anniversaries trying to be happy. But after her fight with Marcus and her conversation with Rita, she was beginning to wonder what else she had missed. She thought for a while, but she couldn't think of an answer that satisfied her. 'I don't know ... to see who else shows up?'

Rita laughed, keeping her eyes closed. 'That's one way to put it. But it's not about seeing how popular I was in life or whatever, it's not even about being remembered. I do it to check up on people, see how they're doing.'

'Ok?' Olive said, still not sure what any of this has to do with her.

Rita sighed and turned towards the door, jerking her head in its direction. 'Look, just come with me. It'll make sense soon, I promise.'

Olive followed her outside. Rita's body had been buried in the town where they spent their afterlife, but it was still quicker to let Gaia's magic guide them. The forest stayed relatively the same, even as they exited Gaia's domain; the tall oaks became gradually shorter and the grass neatly trimmed. More evidence of human life showed up in littered plastic and paper cups, things tossed aside in a moment of carelessness. Gaia would hate that.

Eventually a path appeared, a dirt track that was well-worn. Olive and Rita followed it along until they could see the wrought-iron gate of the cemetery. There were cars parked along the road beside it, and a few people bearing flowers, some wearing all black. There were a lot of people, mostly younger, wandering around. Some of them stood behind the gravestones, looking about as if waiting for someone. Others wandered aimlessly, staring into the faces of people who didn't react to them and then moving away. Rita led Olive past the first few rows of gravestones, going deeper into the yard until they had reached a space that felt isolated, away from the public eye, more a part of nature than of society. There was a fence marking the back of the cemetery, and Rita took Olive over to lean against it.

'Which one's yours?' Olive asked, scanning the graves nearest to them for her name. It hadn't even occurred to Olive until that moment, but had Rita been buried with her dead name on her grave?

Rita raised her arm and pointed to a simple tombstone, a fair distance from where they were. Olive couldn't read the name from where she stood, but she could see that there were flowers there, big orange dahlias. She made a mental note to include those next time she made a bouquet.

'Are we ... going to go see it?' Olive asked, but Rita put a hand on her shoulder.

'Wait.'

A few more people had started appearing, some silent as they stood in front of the graves of their loved ones, others speaking. Some of the people that Olive had noticed before, the wanderers, spoke back to the mourners, weeping joyfully. But the mourners didn't react to them, continuing to speak to the grave markers. Olive took in the outdated outfits and hairstyles of these wanderers, and it dawned on her. These were ghosts, too. 'Are they …?'

Rita nodded, her eyes still fixed on her grave. 'They're dead like us. Some of them do what I do, only come here when they know their loved ones will be here, too. But I think some of the others are stuck here. They can't leave. Or they won't, I guess.'

Olive watched as one of the ghosts fell to their knees, wailing and clawing at their hair while the woman in front of them cried silently, oblivious to their presence. 'That's so sad,' Rita nodded again, chewing her lip. She didn't say anything else for a while, and Olive was left to watch the heartbreaking display of mourners, both dead and alive, trying to make any kind of contact with each other. It wasn't all awful, some of it was actually quite sweet. A living woman was reading out loud from what looked like a diary, and the ghost behind the grave sat on the ground with her legs crossed, smiling and looking up at her with tears in her eyes. But some ghosts paced listlessly, waiting alone. It made Olive wonder what happened to ghosts when there was no one around to remember who they were.

Rita shifted suddenly, a tiny shift forward, but it was enough for Olive to know that she had seen what they came there for. Olive followed her gaze. Making their way slowly across the cemetery were two old women. The taller one had long grey hair and her thin body was almost completely covered by a large overcoat. She had an arm wrapped comfortingly around the shorter one, a small black woman with short white curls and a pair of round glasses that covered half of her face. She was weeping before she saw Rita's gravestone, holding a bunch of orange daisies. This had to be Carla.

'They're married, you know.' Rita said quietly. Olive looked over at her, half expecting to see a face full of jealousy, but instead she wore a proud smile.

'That's amazing,' Olive replied faintly. She hoped it was the right response. Rita seemed glad, her smile getting wider.

'It really is. We never thought we'd see the day when gay couples *could* get married.' she laughed. 'Well, I guess I didn't. But I'm glad she did. It seems like it was worth the wait.'

Olive glanced at Carla and her wife, then back at Rita. 'Do you feel jealous? Because it wasn't you?'

Rita scoffed. 'That's a real loaded question, Olly. Of course I wish I could have married her, but … look at them!'

Olive did. Carla looked to be telling some kind of funny story, laughing through her tears and covering her mouth. Her wife held her close, smiling at her with an expression of absolute adoration.

'They're so happy together.' Rita continued. 'Carla tells me about her every year. I *was* jealous at first, but … but Carla kept saying how much she loved me and how guilty she felt and I …' she paused, a little bit of smoke coming out of her mouth. 'I never want her to feel guilty for being happy. You know if we try to talk to people we knew when we were alive, they don't recognise us?'

Olive shook her head. How could she know that?

'Yeah. It's some sort of mental block, stops them seeing us and having a meltdown. I know I can't talk to her, but I like to think that she knows I'm ok with her moving on. All I've ever wanted was for her to be happy, and she can't do that if she's hung up on a dead girl.' she paused. This was the closest Olive had ever come to seeing her cry. 'Her name is Anais. She's a baker. Owns her own cake shop now. It's going pretty well, apparently, but Carla's always been an optimist. They have a really good life together.'

Olive bit her lip, nodding. She understood that this was important for Rita, and she appreciated her showing Olive such a personal thing, but she still didn't understand why she was here.

Rita sighed, leaning back heavily onto the fence. 'This isn't interesting to you, I get it,'

Olive tried to protest, 'No, I –'

'There was a point to this, I'm not just dragging you out here to make you feel sorry for me.' She gave Olive a knowing stare, and Olive dropped her gaze. 'I told you I was going to tell you why I'm fine with staying here instead of going back, and it's because of Carla. She's the person who matters the most to me, and she's happy now. I don't want to rip that away from her because I feel like I was cheated.'

'But you *were* cheated!' Olive piped up, unable to stop herself. 'You were so young! You don't know what could have happened, she could have been happy with *you*!'

'*Or* she could have been miserable.' Rita narrowed her eyes, straightening up from the fence and crossing her arms. 'I would hope that's not the case, but it's a possibility. Anything could have happened to us. We could have broken up, either of us could have died a different way, we *don't know.*'

She looked back at the couple with a deep sigh. 'But I *know* she's happy now. That much, I'm certain of. I can't be selfish enough to prevent her living a happy, fulfilling life just so that I can spend maybe a few more years with her. It's not worth it.'

Olive stewed on this while Carla and Anais began to leave. 'So what are you going to do when Gaia wants to send you back?'

Rita smirked, and shrugged. 'I'll have to tell 'em no thanks. I mean, hopefully by that point I'll be able to 'move on' to wherever's next, but if not? I think I'll just stay here.'

Olive thought Rita might have wanted to follow Carla, or at least get close enough to see her properly, but she let her old girlfriend and her new wife leave without saying anything. As soon as the couple walked through the gate, Rita turned and walked away silently, leaving Olive to follow behind her. She caught up quickly. She wanted to reach for Rita's hand, but pulled back at the last second.

'I'm sorry. I get so caught up in what *I* want that I can't see why anyone else would choose differently.' She sighed. 'I guess I still don't understand. But I can see how much it means to you – how much Carla means to you. I'll stop pushing. Promise. I'll let you do your thing and I'll stop asking annoying questions.'

Rita finally smiled. 'You do ask a lot of annoying questions.'

She bumped her arm against Olive's, and Olive leaned into her. She slipped her pale hand into Rita's dark one and they walked like that until their surroundings shifted into Gaia's forest and their house came back into view.

Chapter Seven

Before they could make it to the door, Olive hesitated. 'You go in, Rita, I'll catch up with you soon.'

Rita gave her a quizzical look. 'What are you up to?'

'I'm just going into town for a bit. Check out a few places, see if I can find a token.'

Rita stared at her, hard, before shrugging. 'Alright. You'll be back before tonight though, right?'

'Wouldn't miss it!' Olive gave a wink and then turned back into the forest. She kept walking until the foliage shifted to the pavements and buildings of the town with the farmer's market still going on in the distance. Olive had been thinking about their conversation with Jay all day, and something they had said had stuck in her mind. Jay had mentioned a brother and a mother, the three of them attending the farmer's market together. The living people that Olive saw tended to blur together in her mind, but when she thought about it, Jay did look familiar. And it was possible that she had seen their family there, too. It was a long shot, but she was curious. She needed to know more about Jay, if only to learn more about herself.

She stayed hidden, keeping up her invisibility even as she entered the market. She lurked, feeling like the ghosts in the graveyard walking around without finding who or what they were looking for. She couldn't even guarantee that the brother would show up. She was beginning to give up when someone approached. Olive wished she could definitively recognise him as the boy she had seen years ago, but back then she hadn't been paying much attention to anything but the tokens.

He looked like she remembered him. He had the same black hair, golden skin and black-brown eyes as Jay, which made her hopeful. His hair was short, but stood up at odd angles. He looked a lot older than she remembered, but that's because he was. He looked to be about her age now. He wore a heavy black jacket over a red shirt and black denim jeans that were probably a size too big for him, even in the humid weather. His hands were shoved deep into his jacket pockets, and he kept his head low, his expression angry. From what Olive could see of his face, he was quite good looking, but he was glaring forward intently as if trying to ward away any attention.

Olive realised with a jolt that this was the boy who had been watching her the last time she was here. Her curiosity deepened and she kept a close eye on him. Still invisible, she followed him, trying to gather some meaning from the objects he paused at before moving on. She thought that maybe she would be able to tell if he was looking for something to buy for Jay, but he seemed more like he was passing time rather than searching for something specific. He looked in her direction a few times with an annoyed look, but Olive had come to assume that was his default expression.

After a while he started moving faster, taking erratic turns through the rows of stalls. Olive still followed him, her curiosity building. He stopped suddenly and whirled around to stare straight at Olive. She flinched, stepping back, and noticed in the sunlight that his eyes had a pale blue-green reflective tint, the way animals' eyes shone in the dark. She froze, gasping. 'You can see me.'

Frowning at her odd phrase, he took in her appearance and the very public place they were in. He very slowly lowered his chin in a nod, and then inclined his head to the side, to a clearing at the edge of the forest. Taking his lead, Olive followed him. He walked with purpose, taking very decisive steps until he decided they were safely out of anyone's earshot and stopped suddenly, pivoting on his feet to face her again. He did not look happy.

'You're a ghost. I've seen you before.' the sentences could have easily been questions, but he wasn't waiting for an answer. His voice had the same slight rasp that Jay's had, and he kept it quiet even though no one was near enough to hear. 'You've been following me. Why?'

Olive crossed her arms, narrowing her eyes. 'You're a hunter. Have you got your weapon on you?'

The boy glared, his jaw clenching. 'I asked you a question. Why are you following me?'

Seeing she wouldn't make any progress by arguing, Olive blew a lock of hair away from her face. 'Are you Levi? I know Jay. They told me about you.'

At the mention of Jay, the boy stepped back, eyes wide. 'What do you mean you know Jay? How is that possible?'

Olive felt a small smile on her lips. Now she was getting somewhere. 'I've been wondering the same thing, actually. Jay's alive, aren't they? So why can they see ghosts in their dreams?'

Levi frowned in confusion, his head bent low. He took a few deep breaths. 'So that's what's been going on ...'

Olive stepped closer to him, tilting her head, trying to get him to meet her eyes. 'You know something, don't you? What happened to them, on the night of the accident?'

Levi shook his head, exhaling slowly. 'I can't tell you that until you promise me that you won't do anything to hurt Jay.'

Olive frowned. 'What are you talking about? We're just ghosts, we're not monsters.'

'Oh, so there's more of you? Great,' he grumbled.

'Hey, speaking of not hurting people ...' Olive raised an eyebrow. 'You're not carrying a weapon, are you? Not going to slay me after we finish talking?'

After a long pause and eyes that wouldn't stay still, Levi sighed. 'I'm off duty.'

Olive smiled coyly. That was the closest thing to a joke he had said yet, and it had looked like it pained him to say it. 'Good to know. I promise, I won't do anything to hurt

Jay, and neither will any of my friends. I'm Olive, by the way.'

She stuck out her hand, and he gave her a look that was pissed off and confused at the same time. 'You want me to shake your hand?'

Olive nodded with a grin, not lowering her hand. 'That's how people make deals, right? That's what I've read, anyway.'

Levi's expression turned towards the suspicious side. 'You're talking like you're not a person. You ... you *were* a person at some point, right?'

Olive put her hand down, rolling her eyes with exaggeration. 'I don't have any memories from when I was alive. It's a long story.'

Levi blinked a few times. 'Ok then ... so you're saying Jay has just been hanging around with ghosts in their dreams since the accident?'

'Not since the accident. Only the last two nights.' Olive said brightly. 'We've been having a lot of fun. They're going to teach us how to use phones tonight.'

What could have been a faint smile made its way onto Levi's face. 'Of course they are.'

He looked Olive up and down, scanning her face. 'What happened to Jay ... it's complicated. I'm going to need you to hear me out before you respond to anything, ok? Just listen.'

Chapter Eight

Jay hadn't just lost their memories the night of the storm. There were a lot of internal and external injuries that Levi couldn't remember, but that wasn't all. Jay didn't just have a near-death experience – they had actually died.

Levi heard the tree crash to the ground in his sleep, but when he woke up he found himself not in his tent, but underwater. In the moment he thought it was a dream. He was hovering upright in this dark greenish water, but when he looked down at himself his clothes and hair were dry. He looked around, and with a shock of revulsion, he saw Jay floating behind him, their eyes closed, dark tendrils coming up from deep below to wrap around their ankles and wrists.

He tried to swim towards them, but he couldn't get any closer than he already was. Panicking, he looked around wildly, and saw a dark shape beginning to form. A mess of algae from deep below the water, well past the point where Levi's eyes could see, rose like a tower. The tangle of shadows that was gathering before his eyes slowly shifted into a vaguely humanoid shape. A horrible amphibious creature stood before him, tethered to the bottom of the water, a mockery of the human body with all the features of a crocodile. The thing gave a terribly toothy grin as it opened its cold, lifeless eyes.

'This one … this is your family, correct?' The thing spoke in a voice that chilled Levi to the bone. It gestured a slimy hand toward Jay, who was still unresponsive.

Rage boiled up in Levi's chest, and he found his voice. 'What have you done to them?'

The thing made a sound like it was choking, which Levi quickly realised was a terrible cackle. 'I haven't done anything! The predicament they're in now is the fault of the tree that fell on them. Or the terrible decision to go camping during a storm. Take your pick.'

Levi was slowly processing what was going on, and he didn't like any of it. 'Let them go,' he wasn't exactly sure what he was going to do if they didn't.

'I'm surprised to see you here. You usually have to be dead like this one to come to this place, but ...' it cut off when it saw Levi's terrified expression. 'Oh ... you don't know who you are, do you? That's curious ... did your parents not tell you? Do you not see people who aren't there? Never had an imaginary friend that seemed a bit too real?'

'Stop playing games, just tell me what you want!'

'I was getting there.' the thing said, a note of impatience making their voice sharp. 'This one that you're so concerned with, I got to their soul first, which means that they belong to me now.'

It waved its arm and Levi suddenly saw a multitude of transparent black shadows darting around. Levi could hear them screaming. 'This can't be happening. They can't be dead.'

The thing grinned wider. 'Ah, but they are. And since I reached them just in time, they'll join the rest of the souls down here with me.'

Levi felt panic choking up in his throat. He watched the shadows wrap round his sibling, who was completely still. There was not even a rising and falling of their chest to indicate that they were breathing. They looked so fragile floating there, much younger than they really were. He had let this happen. He had promised to take care of them, promised their mother that he would keep them safe, and he had failed. 'There has to be another way. They're too young to die!'

A deep rumble came from the reptilian creature's throat. 'Lots of people die young. Much younger than this by far. What makes this one so special?'

'Take me instead.'

The words were out of his mouth before he could stop them. He watched the creature's face freeze, its eyes unblinking. 'I'll take their place if you let them live.'

The thing lowered slightly in the water, like a crocodile getting ready to spring on its prey. 'I suppose it is ... *convenient* that you showed up here. I can't take your soul while you're still alive, my powers aren't that great.' the scaly lips split into a grin so wide that the corners looked like they were about to rip open. 'But maybe a deal can be made?'

Levi froze, looking back at Jay's lifeless body. 'What do you need me to do?'

'Do you understand what I mean when I tell you that you are a hunter?' the thing asked, looking at him expectantly. Levi kept glancing anxiously at Jay, dreading that something would happen to them while the two were talking meaninglessly. He didn't say anything, just shook his head.

The thing's head tilted. 'You're able to see me. I'm willing to guess that you have been able to see ghosts all your life, though you may not have been aware that that's what they are. People that only you seem to see? Yes?'

Levi narrowed his eyes. He was aware that he saw people that weren't there. He had been diagnosed with schizophrenia a few years ago, but he had been having hallucinations for a long time before that. Not all of his symptoms could be explained away by the presence of ghosts, though, so he couldn't be sure that the creature wasn't trying to trick him into something.

'Don't believe me? Ask your parents. These things are usually passed down through blood. You're a hunter, boy, whether you accept it or not. There is a long history of people like you hunting down stray ghosts and sending them on their way. I'm surprised you aren't already aware of this; most hunter families train their children as soon as they can hold a weapon.'

'If that's true,' Levi said, clenching his jaw. 'Why shouldn't I kill you right now?'

The thing cackled again, the sound grating Levi's ears. 'I'd like to see you try, without a weapon! No, you would need a very specific weapon to destroy me. Someone in your family will have one. These are powerful things, forged from an ancient magic born of the spiritual realm. If you find this weapon, you can use it to help me, and I will let your sibling live.'

Levi frowned. 'How can it help *you*? Do you ... do you *want* to move on from here?'

Laughter again from the creature. 'Oh, no, that's the last thing I want. I'm quite happy here. No, I want you to take this,' it clasped its hands together, its webbed fingers making a horrible wet sound. A light emanated from the hands, and when it opened them, there was what looked like a flickering orb of fire, but the flames were a deep turquoise, and the centre was black. 'I need you to imbue this into your weapon, so that when you slay a ghost, their soul will belong to me.'

Levi stared at the orb, the lights dazzling his eyes and pulling him into a trance. 'How am I supposed to kill a ghost?'

The creature sighed, growing bored with the conversation. 'Ask your family. Find other hunters, if you have to. I'm not in any rush. I've waited this long, after all.'

'And … and if I take that from you, you'll let Jay go?'

The creature held out the orb, its face inscrutable. 'It's a deal.'

Levi reached out. As soon as his hand came near the flames, he felt a burst of ice-cold pain shoot up his arm, more intense than anything he had felt before. He cried out, but there was a sound like rushing water so heavy in his ears and a flash of light so bright that he couldn't focus on anything except the pain. The light overtook him until it had faded to black, and he felt the rain and the wind from the night's storm pelting down on him.

His one-person tent had collapsed on top of him. He felt strangled beneath the canvas and his sleeping bag, feeling his chest tighten as he scrambled to free himself. He cried out Jay's name until he felt his throat grow hoarse. He tried to get his bearings, but it was difficult with the storm raging above him. He saw a massive oak tree uprooted, lying horizontal on the ground, and from underneath it he spotted the canvas of Jay's tent.

His vision blurred as he rushed towards the tree, his limbs shaking. He tried to move the tree, but it was far too heavy for him to lift. He jumped over the trunk and landed on the other side, where he could see a shape underneath the tent. He tried to find a zip, a tear, any possible way to get the tent open, but he couldn't. His mind ticked over at double speed as he tried to decide whether he should stay there and keep fumbling with the tent, or risk leaving to grab the knife from his bag to cut it open. Every second he wasted was another second Jay could be dying, and he wasn't about to risk their life on a deal with a monster he couldn't guarantee wasn't another hallucination.

He made up his mind to dash to his tent, rummaging through his bag as quickly as he could to find his knife, and on a last-second whim, he dug out his phone as well. He set to work cutting away at the tent, careful to stay away from Jay's body. Every time the knife slipped against the wet fabric he grew more frustrated and impatient, and his movements became more clumsy and panicked. Far too much time had passed before he was able to rip the tent away from where the tree had pinned it to Jay's waist. He couldn't see their legs underneath the trunk of the oak, but he was able to see their face at last. Rain mixed with the tears on his cheeks as he held one of his hands underneath their nose, feeling the faintest breath. Snapping out of his relief, he checked for a pulse, trying not to gag at the scent of the blood on their face and arms.

Feeling a faint thumping in their neck, Levi stepped back and called an ambulance. The responder stayed on the line with him until they arrived, and then everything was a blur. He barely registered anything that was being said to him, barely felt the shock blanket around his shoulders. He kept his eyes on Jay the whole time, and only once they were well on their way to the hospital did he make the dreaded phone call to their mother.

***

'Can you bring my comic books? The older ones, in the box under my bed?'

Jay was still looking fragile, with tubes and needles sticking out of them, but at least they were talking. At least they were alive.

Levi scrunched up his nose, flicking his fingernails against their bedpost. 'You want me to look under *your* bed? There's got to be about a dozen rats under there, at least.'

Jay rolled their eyes with an exaggerated groan. 'Shut up, it's not that bad. You can try and find my DS too, while you're at it.'

'You haven't used that thing in years.'

'Then I guess I have a lot of catching up to do.' They gave him a cold glare to remind him that yes, they had lost their memories.

Levi felt a twinge of guilt. He kept slipping up, believing for a minute that things were the same as they'd always been, but then he would remember that his reality was a few steps ahead of Jay's. He felt useless here. There was nothing he could do to make their time here any easier, nothing he could say to reassure them that they would be fine. The doctors had warned that Jay's memories might never recover, at least completely, and the idea terrified him. He may have stopped them from dying, but they would never get their life back to the way it was.

There were so many pieces of them that he cherished so closely in his mind, but were now lost to time. Those awkward pre-teen years that Levi remembered as being nothing but embarrassing were incredibly important in shaping Jay's identity, and now those memories were gone. All of the friends they'd made in middle school, discovering they didn't fit into the gender binary, choosing a new name, cutting their hair short and then growing it out again ... Jay remembered none of it. They were still the same person, Levi had to keep reminding himself. They still acted the same, still pestered Levi and pretended to be annoyed by their mother Nhi, like they always had.

It was Levi that was missing something. If events and memories were a series of strings, all connected to each other in different ways, stretching across time, then the years that Jay had forgotten had been snipped away from the rest, floating in isolation. There were so many memories that used to belong to the two of them, but now they were Levi's to carry alone, and they felt like heavy secrets that he was forbidden to speak about. Telling awful ghost stories by the campfire, Jay playing video games while Levi was studying, sneaking them a sip of champagne at his graduation, sitting on their bed and confiding that he might be having feelings for guys. These weren't shared memories anymore.

He saw how frustrated it made Jay when their friends showed up with photos, pressuring them to remember. It wasn't fair to bring those memories up, so they remained locked up tightly in his mind.

The door to the room flung open and their mother, Nhi, burst in wielding a brown paper takeaway bag and a flustered expression. 'Sorry I took so long, you wouldn't *believe* how busy it was in there!'

Jay grinned as she started handing out burgers wrapped in greasy paper and packets of fries, saving a chicken wrap for herself. 'Thanks, mum!'

Nhi breathed a world-weary sigh and got herself situated on the edge of Jay's bed, looking at them with glowing admiration. 'We're so proud of you, you know that? You're doing so well.'

Jay dug into their burger, getting sauce all over their face. Levi could see how hard it was for Nhi to hold herself back from wiping it off. 'I don't know what there is to be proud of. I'm not doing much of *anything* right now.'

Levi wanted to tell them that they were being good and not complaining, but even that wasn't true. He wasn't going to tell them that, though. He felt an obligation to be nice to them. 'You're surviving. You kicked death's ass, if that isn't something to be proud of, I don't know what is.'

'Stayin' alive out of spite,' Jay laughed. 'That sounds pretty on-brand for me. You guys had better hurry up and eat, you know how strict the nurses are about visiting hours.'

Nhi leaned heavily against Jay, being careful of their tubes, and rested her cheek on their shoulder. 'I don't want to leave my baby alone again.'

Jay snorted and tried to shove her away. 'Mum, I'll be *fine!* I'll just be sleeping anyway. Besides, Levi's got a whole list of things he's got to bring back for me tomorrow.'

'Not likely,' Levi muttered, smiling, though he had every intention of doing what they had asked him to. 'Jay's right though, mum, we need our rest too.'

He stood from his cold metal chair and put a hand on his mother's shoulder. She was looking more tired than Jay did, with dark bags forming under her eyes and an exhausted air to everything she did. Levi knew she hadn't slept since the accident, and she moved through the regular motions of her day in a robotic, zombie-like trance. Levi had moved out of home and into a small, crowded apartment a year ago, but he went back to his old room after the accident. Someone needed to be there to comfort Nhi and make sure she didn't do anything reckless. Nhi tried to keep both of their spirits high, but the house felt empty and heavy without Jay there, their absence creating a palpable tension. Levi couldn't help feeling like her unhappiness was his fault, like there was something more he should be doing. He had saved Jay's life, hadn't he? So what was he feeling so guilty about?

Nhi gave Jay a weepy hug, keeping up her very complicated act of pretending to be more upset than she was, while actually being more distraught than she would ever let on. She wasn't a very good actor, but she didn't seem to realise how transparent she was being.

Nhi stepped aside and Levi went in for a hug. He was glad to feel the warmth of their skin, but his mind flashed back to the woods when he had found them unconscious, desperately searching for a pulse. 'Try not to get too bored in here, ok?'

Jay exhaled heavily. Levi could tell they were trying to think of something snarky to say, but they just looked exhausted. 'Yeah … I guess I'll just go back to sleep. Again.'

Levi laughed lightly, trying not to disrupt them. He and Nhi left the hospital room, and Nhi immediately started sniffling. Levi put his arm around her shoulders, suddenly aware of how small she really was compared to him. She retrieved a tissue from the pocket of her jeans and blew her nose quietly, politely, as they walked out of the front doors. 'I feel like such a bad mother.'

Levi stopped in his tracks, pulling Nhi to a stop beside him. 'Why would you say that?'

Nhi covered her face with her hands. 'What kind of mother lets her children go camping in a storm?'

'Mum, that storm came out of nowhere, no one could have known it was going to get that bad.' Levi took a breath, preparing to say the thing he had avoided thinking about. 'It's my fault. They wanted me to go, but I should have just said no. I made myself responsible for them when I agreed to go, and I let them down.'

Levi hadn't even planned on going this year. He was still adjusting to his life away from home, balancing his studies and work, and he had avoided telling Jay that he wouldn't be able to make it. But they begged him to come anyway, and he remembered how much he missed seeing their face every day, and he was convinced. All he had to have done was stay firm, stick with his excuses, and none of this would have happened. Not the accident, not Jay's death, not the encounter with the ghostly amphibian that he still couldn't explain.

'Oh, sweetheart …' Nhi turned and wrapped him in a hug. 'We shouldn't blame ourselves, I'm sorry. These things happen. It's awful, but they happen! It's a miracle they survived, we should be celebrating that!'

Levi patted her back until she let go. 'C'mon, let's go home. I'll make some tea.'

Nhi smiled brightly, her eyes shining beneath unshed tears. 'You're a good boy, you really are. You take good care of your family.'

When they reached the parking lot, Levi tried to get into the driver's side, but Nhi batted his arm.

'Mum, I can drive.' Levi said firmly. She was clearly distracted, it might have been good for her to just sleep, but she waved him off.

'No, no, I'm fine. Just make sure you talk to me, I need something to keep my mind on.'

That was not what Levi had wanted to hear. He had been hoping for a quiet drive where he could just focus on the road ahead and nothing else. Forcing himself to make conversation when he had no energy for talking did not appeal to him. But his mother could be very stubborn when she wanted to be, so he let her take the wheel.

There was actually something he needed to ask her about. He felt like that moment may not have been the right place for it, but in a sense, there was no better time to do it. He had read somewhere that car rides were the best place for difficult conversations. Something about having a destination and a clear end to the conversation. He hoped that was true.

'Hey mum ... there's something I want to ask you,' he said as he buckled himself into the passenger seat.

Nhi started the car, going through the motions but showing a bit of concern. 'What is it, sweetie?'

Levi took a few deep breaths. How did you just come out and ask your mother if your family was part of a long line of ghost hunters? 'Uh ... this is going to sound weird. I'm not really sure how to ask this ...'

Nhi gave him a sympathetic look as she prepared to reverse out of the park. 'It's ok honey, you know you can ask me anything,'

Levi sighed. This definitely was not the awkward parent-child conversation that Nhi no doubt thought it was. He tried to think of a way to slowly introduce the topic, make it have some kind of relevance before springing the whole ghost thing on her out of nowhere. 'Do you ... do you know if there's another reason I have hallucinations?'

Nhi went silent, her gaze becoming glassy in the reflections of the mirrors. 'I know ... that it's been difficult for you, but we finally have a diagnosis now! You're starting to get the help you need and – and if this doctor isn't working for you we can always try someone else.'

'Yeah, it's ... it's great that I can finally put a name to it,' Levi had hoped his mum would take the conversation from there, but it was clear she wouldn't give him the answers he wanted unless he asked directly. 'But I've been doing a bit of research. You know how I've been seeing people my whole life? For as long as I can remember? Well, apparently it's rare for symptoms of schizophrenia to show up earlier than eighteen, and even rarer from under thirteen.'

Nhi's voice got very quiet. 'Just ask me what it is you want to ask me.'

Levi paused, taken aback by the coldness in her tone. 'I just ... look, there's something else going on here, isn't there? And it's not just me, is it? It's our family. Does Dad see them too? Or ... or is it you?'

Nhi seemed to deflate, keeping her eyes locked straight ahead on the road. 'I was trying to avoid this ... you found out, didn't you? Did one of them speak to you?'

He had to think about this. He had wanted to see if what the swamp spirit had said was true, but he wasn't sure if he wanted to tell his mother about it just yet. 'Yes. I ... saw one at the market and they told me that ... that I was a hunter. Is it true?'

'Levi, honey, it's ...' she sighed deeply. 'Yes, it's true. I wanted to protect the two of you, let you live normal lives. And before you get upset, I know it wasn't fair! I just ... I had this hope that you wouldn't notice anything different about the ghosts. I don't want you to think that I was taking advantage of your ... of your condition, because that's not it! I couldn't plan for that.'

Levi felt a flash of hurt at the way she'd framed it. 'You were using my schizophrenia as a scapegoat? Because it was *convenient?*'

'It wasn't like that!' she protested. 'I knew you needed help that I couldn't give you. And I *got* you help, didn't I?

Didn't we go through all those psychiatrists and doctors to figure it out?'

She was getting distressed. Levi silently cursed himself. He felt that he had a right to be angry, but Nhi didn't need more reasons to feel like she had failed as a parent.

His mother stifled a sob, then took a deep breath to steady herself. 'I'm sorry. I have so many things to apologise for, I know I do. When you were growing up, I just remembered how hard it was for me to make friends with other people my age and to feel *normal,* but ...' she finally looked at him, a brief, heartbreaking glance. 'I tried my best with you, I really did. But I made so many mistakes anyway.'

Levi turned his towards the window, but he wasn't really paying attention to anything outside of it. He had to stop himself from consoling her, telling her that everything was alright. Because it wasn't. She had lied to him about *huge* parts of his life.

But he needed to know more, so he couldn't say what he wanted to. 'How come I can see them, and Jay can't?'

'It usually only happens to one person in the family, I don't know why. Usually the oldest.'

'Did Dad know you could see them?'

Nhi bit her lip, her shoulders tensing. 'Not ... at first. I didn't want to scare him off, but then we had you, and I knew it would only be a matter of time before the signs started showing and I'd have a lot of explaining to do. I thought he had taken it well at the time, but ...'

Levi's heart skipped a beat. 'Is that why he left? Because of me?'

'Oh, honey, no!' all the emotion returned to Nhi's voice at once. 'Don't *ever* think that it's your fault! I should have been honest with him from the start, but ... we were having issues long before then. I'm so sorry that I kept this from you. I *swear* I was planning on telling you, but you've been so busy with moving, and finishing school before that, and ...' she sighed. 'I just keep making excuses. But that's not fair on you. I'm sorry.'

Levi just wanted to sit and absorb this new information, but he could see their street approaching fast and he knew he didn't have long before his mum would walk off and pretend the conversation had never happened. He needed to find someone else who could give him more answers. 'So ... you wouldn't want me to start hunting ghosts?'

Nhi shook her head. 'No. It's dangerous work, Levi, and there's no reward. Most ghosts can't actually hurt living people, but they *can* hurt us. That's why I've always told you not to interact with the people you saw, because if they felt threatened they could have attacked you. You have to promise me that you won't talk to any of them, alright? Even if they seem harmless, they aren't. The ghosts that you'll usually see aren't dangerous unless provoked but … but there are other things like them, other kinds of dead people that only want to hurt the living. *That's* why hunters exist, so that we can protect each other.'

'If that's true, then isn't it my responsibility to be a hunter?'

Nhi's brow furrowed and she looked pained. 'I don't know. You didn't get to choose this. You shouldn't be *responsible* for anything like that.'

'Do you know any other hunters? Do *I* know any?'

Nhi swallowed hard, then nodded quickly, distractedly. 'Most of my friends are hunters. I don't see a lot of them anymore, they move around a lot. They're much more dedicated to the cause than I am, I'm unofficially retired from hunting. But there are a few I still see. Rami's one. And his daughter. You know, the older one? She's got the purple hair now?'

'Shivan?' Levi couldn't believe this. He had known Rami and his family for as long as he could remember. They were family friends. He'd gone to high school with Shivan's younger sister, Daya. Levi wouldn't have described them as 'normal', exactly, but he definitely wouldn't have thought of them as ghost hunters. That *did* give him a starting point, though. He hadn't properly caught up with Shivan since he finished high school, but he was sure she would be happy to meet up with him. Whether she would tell him what he wanted to know was a different question.

There was something else he needed to know. 'What did you use to fight the ghosts?'

Nhi sighed as she spun the wheel, pulling into their driveway. 'A sword. The one you kept begging me to use as a kid,'

'And you hid it in a box in the basement.' Levi recalled. 'Yeah, I know the one.'

Nhi stopped the car, unbuckled her seatbelt and turned to look him dead in the eye. 'I'm sorry that I kept this a secret from you for so long. And I understand if you're upset, and if you feel tempted to get involved,' she held his gaze steadily, 'but this doesn't have to be a part of your life.

You can ignore this. You can be *safe*. I *need* you and Jay to be safe. They don't need to know about any of this.'

Levi met her gaze and held it, trying for a smile. 'I won't tell them, ok? I'll stay safe.'

Inside, Levi brewed a pot of tea like he had promised, but he was preoccupied. While he was pouring the tea, he heard a voice that sounded eerily similar to the devilish swamp spirit and he glanced around for it, overfilling one of the cups and spilling jasmine tea all over the countertop. He quickly grabbed a cloth to mop it up with, but his mind was just as close to overflowing. He hadn't heard the thing's voice since the night of the accident, so it could have easily been a hallucination, the same as he'd always had. But he had made a deal with the thing, hadn't he? Did that mean it could speak through his mind?

He carried the tray with the teapot and cup into the living room, cringing as he realised it would have been much easier to pour the cup *after* he had put the tray down. A little bit of tea spilled over the edges.

Nhi looked up when he walked in, looking like she had been falling asleep in her armchair. 'You're not having one?' she asked, noticing the single cup.

Levi shook his head. 'Nah, I've got some studying to do.'

Nhi held the teacup in both hands, breathing in the steam. 'Are you sure you can't take a night off? You shouldn't overwork yourself.'

'I just have a few things I need to finish before tomorrow. It'll be fine.'

Levi was counting on that pot of tea to last Nhi an hour, at least. Instead of going to his room to study, he went into the laundry, where the trapdoor to the attic swung down from the ceiling. He pulled the cord and climbed up the staircase. His mother didn't like to throw anything away, but she was also notoriously disorganised, so the attic space was a complete mess. There were cardboard boxes packed to the brim with old toys and clothes, magazines and VHS tapes, Jay's old comics that they'd long forgotten about but would be angry to know were up here.

Levi knew what he was looking for, even among the chaos. It was the only thing not in a cardboard box, though it was covered in a thick layer of dust. Levi found the long black wooden box at the back of the attic, behind a pile of old photo albums. He pulled the lid off. The sword was exactly as he had remembered it, a Vietnamese *Kiem* with a thin, straight blade and an intricately carved hilt. Nhi used to have it mounted over the mantlepiece in the living room, a family heirloom that reminded her and her children of their heritage. But now, knowing what he did, Levi was sure it was a reminder of other things, too.

He untied the leather straps that held it in place in its box and lifted it into his hands, feeling its weight. Despite being fascinated with it all his life, he had never touched it before, and it was lighter than he had expected. As he held it, one hand under the hilt and the other under the blade, he heard faint rustling whispers. The hand under the hilt began glowing, first white, and then teal, until it darkened to almost black, and the whispers increased in volume until they surrounded his mind like a swarm of angry wasps. He dropped the sword and jolted backwards in shock, and both the glowing and the whispers subsided.

So it hadn't been a dream, his encounter with the swamp creature. He could have brushed it off as another hallucination, but he could still feel a burning sensation in the palm of his hand. Very cautiously, he picked up the sword again and placed it back in its box, strapping it back in.

His hands shaking, he pulled his phone from his pocket and dialled Shivan's number. The phone rang for a long time, but finally she picked up.

'Is that actually you, Levi?' her voice came through the receiver much louder than he was expecting, and he winced.

'Yep, sure is.'

'God, I haven't heard from you in ages. We thought you'd *died* or something.'

Levi was glad no one was there to see him roll his eyes at the irony of that statement. 'I told you I was moving. I've been really busy.'

'I know, I remember what it was like leaving home for the first time. You're making me feel so old! It only seems like yesterday that you were starting high school.'

'You're only two years older than me.'

'Yes, but those two extra years are full of wisdom and experience.' she said, dramatically cryptic. 'Anyway, what's up?'

Levi swallowed. 'There's uh ... there's something I want to talk to you about. Something important.'

He had expected her to make a joke, but she fell silent. Levi was about to say something, unsure if the line had gone dead, when she spoke up again. 'Wow, ok. I think I know what this is about. Well, me and Bee are around tomorrow morning if you want to stop by for a coffee or something?'

Levi looked at the palm of his hand, and then back at the box that held the sword, certain for a second that he had seen a turquoise light around it. 'Huh? Oh, yeah. Tomorrow works fine.'

'Ok then. See you soon.'

'Bye.'

Levi breathed a sigh of relief after he hung up. He always dreaded making phone calls, and he felt especially guilty that he hadn't called sooner. He hated that he'd only contacted Shivan when he needed something from her, but what else was he supposed to do? He needed to know more about being a hunter so that he could either make good on his promise to the swamp creature and set Jay free for good, or find a way to destroy the thing himself. But now that he knew that ghosts could hurt hunters, he needed to know how to protect himself as well as Jay.

If Shivan really was a hunter, she would be able to help him, but that would mean keeping it a secret from Nhi.

Levi felt terrible going around behind his mother's back like this, but he didn't see another option.

***

Shivan and her girlfriend, Bianca, lived in a dingy apartment in the middle of the city. Shivan greeted him at the door with a strong high-five that turned into a one-armed hug. She packed a lot of power into her tiny frame. Since she'd left high school, she had made a lot of changes to her appearance. She had a stud with a black gem in her nose, and a ring in her left eyebrow. Her hair used to be dark brown and silky smooth, but after years of dying it, it had become frayed and bleached, and it was currently a slightly faded blue-violet. She wore a lot of denim now, and handmade jewellery.

'Good to see you, Shiv,' he said.

'Good to see you too, man,' she grinned up at him.

Bianca appeared in the doorway, giving him a mellow wave. She was much taller than Shivan, and more muscular. While Shivan always dressed like she threw on whatever clothes she pulled from the floor of her wardrobe, Bianca was always very well put-together. Even her wine-red bob never had a hair out of place. She slid an arm around Shivan's shoulder and smiled at Levi with her lips closed.

'Sorry to barge in on you like this,' he said, stepping to the small kitchen.

Shivan bounced over to flick on the electric kettle and took a seat while Bianca set out the mugs. 'What are you sorry for? We're glad to see you, aren't we, Bee?'

'Sure are,' Bianca said in her low voice, her deep burgundy lips pulled up in the slightest smirk. Levi thought she looked mildly amused, but she was always difficult to read.

'How's Jay? Are they holding up alright?' she asked, and Shivan leaned in, looking interested.

Levi broke away from their gaze and found his own place at the table. 'Yeah, they're better. Getting used to the hospital and everything.'

Shivan gave him a sympathetic look. 'Do they remember anything? I know you must be sick of answering this ...'

Levi shook his head. 'It's fine. No, they still don't remember, but they're dealing with it. I think they're handling it pretty well.'

Bianca nodded gently. 'I'm sure they are. They're stronger than they know.'

Shivan pulled her legs up under her until she was hunched on her chair like a gargoyle. She seemed to pick up on Levi's nerves, and his hesitation to broach the subject that had brought him here. 'So, what did you want to talk about?'

Levi was hit with the sudden fear that he was wrong about Shivan being a hunter, and that what he was about to say was going to make no sense. But he did not want to dance around the topic like he had with his mother, so he said it anyway. 'I know about the ghost hunting thing.'

Shivan grinned wide, the gem in her nose flashing. 'What did I tell you, Bee? See, I knew he'd figure it out eventually!'

She punched him lightly on the arm. Bianca raised an eyebrow, humming in half-hearted agreeance as she placed two mugs of instant coffee on the table. Levi gave her a quick nod of thanks before turning back to Shivan. 'Wait, so you knew I was a hunter?'

'Yeah, obviously!' Shivan laughed. 'Your mum made sure me and my dad didn't bring it up. It was pretty obvious, though. You'd be clearly staring right at a ghost and then pretending you didn't see it. It was kind of hilarious, actually.'

'So when did the penny finally drop?' Bianca asked, bringing her own mug over and elbowing Shivan.

'Oh, uh … I guess you were right; I am pretty oblivious. A ghost caught me staring and confronted me about it. I thought it might have been another hallucination, but those don't usually keep up a conversation for too long.' He slipped into the lie more easily than he had planned to. He just wasn't sure how much he should reveal, and what was going to get him in trouble.

'Did you tell your mum?' Shivan said, slurping her coffee.

'Yeah, and she told me all about it. How she was trying to protect me by keeping it a secret.' he blew on his coffee to cool it down. 'It's … funny, you know? I always knew I was weird, and the schizophrenia explained some of it, but now it *really* makes sense.'

'Levi, none of that makes you *weird,*' Bianca said, her eyes steady as she stared at him. 'Just different. I can't speak for your schizophrenia, but people like us are perfectly capable of leading normal lives, if we want.'

Levi blinked. 'People like us? So you're a hunter too?'

She tilted her head with a sly smile. 'Of course. Why do you think Shivan and I get along so well?'

Levi exhaled, rubbing his temple with his fingers. 'Wow. This is, uh ... this is a lot to process.'

'It's a lot of information to take in at once,' Bianca said with a kind smile. 'It's not as scary as it sounds. It's pretty boring once you know what you're doing.'

'But that's not what you're here for, right?' Shivan piped up. 'It sounds like Nhi was pretty adamant about keeping you away from the whole hunting business. Can't imagine she'd want us to initiate you.'

Levi chewed his lip. Guilt was creeping back into his mind; it was bad enough that he was keeping things from his mother, but now he was asking others to do the same. 'Actually, that is why I'm here. I want to learn as much about hunting as I can. I want you to teach me.'

Shivan and Bianca exchanged a glance. Shivan tapped the handle of her mug with a black fingernail. 'Nhi doesn't know about this at all, huh?'

Levi dropped his eyes. 'No, she doesn't. I know it's not fair to ask you to lie to her, but ... I just really need to know who I am. All of it.'

'This is a big deal to you, isn't it?' Shivan's voice had lost all of its usual playfulness. She sighed, her dark eyes flickering as she struggled to make up her mind. 'I mean, I guess ...You know Nhi is like family to me, right? You and Jay too, of course, but like ... you're asking a lot of me. This goes against what she wanted for you.'

She looked to Bianca for support, but she was staring off into the distance, tight-lipped. Shivan's eyes flickered over Levi's face, and she gave another defeated sigh, her shoulders sinking. 'But on the other hand, we can't really understand what it's been like for you. We've *always* known we were hunters, we did it because it's been this way our entire lives. But you're only finding out about it now, and that's rough.'

Levi looked down and nodded awkwardly, not sure what to say.

Shivan gave a slightly pleading look to her girlfriend, who still didn't offer any insight. 'But I guess that's the difference, right? We didn't get a choice in this, we just accepted it because that was just the way our lives were. You have a *choice* though, right? And sure, maybe you can choose to ignore all the ghost stuff. But if you actually *want* to do this … well, isn't that a choice too? You should be able to decide for yourself.'

Bianca smirked. 'That was very profound, babe. I'm impressed.'

'Right?' Shivan smiled up at Bianca, who planted a kiss on her cheek. 'Anyway. We can definitely teach you, but I want to avoid lying to Nhi as much as possible, ok?'

Levi nodded. 'Yeah, I understand that. I'll come up with something.'

Bianca sipped her tea calmly. 'It doesn't hurt to have another hunter around. Especially considering Jay isn't one.'

Levi frowned. 'What do you mean? Why does that make a difference?'

'You mean Nhi didn't tell you?' Bianca's eyes went wide. 'Ghosts can still attack anyone with hunters' blood, even if they aren't a hunter themselves. They'd still be able to sense it in Jay.'

Levi felt his head grow faint. Jay still wasn't safe, even after everything he had done to keep them out of danger. 'That changes things,'

Shivan put a comforting hand on his arm. 'Yeah, I know. That's why I was so protective of Daya. Even then, I couldn't ...'

She trailed off, giving a nervous laugh as she tried to figure out how to finish the sentence, but no words came.

A dawning realisation came to Levi. Daya had died years ago, when they had just started high school. She was Levi's age. He had always thought that she died in a car crash, but now ...

'Are you telling me ghosts can kill people?' the words were out of his mouth before he could stop them. Shivan looked at him like he'd stabbed her, and Bianca's gaze went cold. He froze and looked down. 'I'm sorry. I just ... I wasn't expecting to hear that.'

'It's fine,' Shivan said with a smile, but she seemed to have shrunk into herself. 'That can't be easy to hear. I know you care about Jay as much as I cared about Daya, so it's a good thing you came to us. If you want to protect them, we can teach you how to do that. Do you have a weapon?'

Levi nodded, though he had barely heard her. He couldn't believe his mother had refused to train him when Jay was in danger as well. How many times had they come close to being hurt? Would it have taken Jay's death for Nhi to tell him the truth, or would she have made up another lie to keep him in the dark? Did she feel any guilt at Daya's funeral, knowing that she had lied about the death of her son's friend so blatantly?

'We can run you through the basics now if you want, but if you bring your weapon next time, we can show you how to use it properly.' Shivan was saying. She noticed him staring intently into his coffee mug and nudged him. 'You doing ok, dude?'

'Huh?' Levi blinked, snapping back into the present moment. 'Yeah, I'm fine. That sounds good.'

She nodded sympathetically, placing her hand on his, and his guilt deepened. 'I understand. It's a lot to take in, right? We'll keep Jay safe with you. I've been meaning to drop in and visit them sometime.'

'How's your mum handling it?' Bianca asked.

'About as well as she can.' Levi sighed. He had really hoped that they'd finished talking about Jay and the hospital earlier, but apparently not.

'We don't have to talk ghosts anymore if you don't want to,' Shivan suggested gently.

'No ... no, I think that's exactly what I need right now. A distraction.'

Shivan looked at him quizzically before continuing. 'Ok, well ... do you have any burning questions before I get into the 101 stuff?'

Levi tried to think. 'Let's start simple. What does it actually mean to hunt a ghost? If they're already dead, what happens to them?'

'Good question.' Bianca said. 'To answer that, we need to clarify what a ghost actually is, first. As far as we know, there are three different realms of reality. The first is ours, the physical or mortal realm. The second is the spiritual realm, which intersects with ours. It's mostly made up of energy, and the beings that inhabit it are elementals, who influence what happens to the natural world of our realm. The third realm is where people go when they die. No one knows exactly what it is, or if it's even a place. It could just be a transitional stage between this life and the next, as far as we know. But sometimes, people get stuck on their way there. They get trapped in the spiritual realm, and *that's* what ghosts are. Mostly it's because they have some unfinished business, but ... I don't have to explain that, right? You've seen just about any ghost movie, right?'

Levi nodded with a slight smile, a little in awe of how quickly she was rattling off this information and trying to keep up with her.

'Yeah, so. Some of them are angry, looking for revenge, etcetera, and that's when they become dangerous. Spirits that are so full of rage that it gives them influence over the physical realm, they're what we call poltergeists. They can hurt people, and that's when we step in. Slaying a ghost with a hunter's weapon sends them straight to the third plane, to face whatever justice they have coming for them.'

'Most ghosts are pretty chill with hanging around until they move on,' Shivan interjected. 'I know it seems like when you're a ghost hunter, you should be trying to slay every ghost you see, but that's not how it works. The ones that aren't poltergeists generally aren't out to hurt anyone, so we can leave them be. Some of them *want* to move on, though, so it's ok to help them out. But, god, can you imagine if we had to slay *every* ghost? We'd never get anything done.'

Levi felt like he should have been taking notes. 'So ... you said there were elementals in the spiritual realm. And there are ghosts. Is there anything else?' Nothing they had said so far explained the swamp creature Levi had made a deal with, unless it happened to be a particularly corrupted poltergeist.

Shivan tilted her head to stare up at the ceiling, humming thoughtfully. 'Well, there was another type of spirit that my dad told me about, but ... I don't know, he said they were just a myth, and we've never come across one before, so it's probably not worth talking about.'

Levi leant forward. 'Can you tell me anyway? I want to be as prepared as possible.'

Shivan gave him a strange look, and he hoped she couldn't see the desperation in his eyes. 'He called them demons. Don't know how accurate that is, but not much is known about them, so it's the best we've got. I'll tell you, but don't get too caught up in them, ok? Don't let it scare you.'

He raised an eyebrow at her. 'I think I can handle it.'

She shrugged with a wry smile, issuing a challenge. 'These demons look like they could be elementals, but they're not from the spiritual realm. They used to be human. Not only that, but they used to be hunters.'

She paused for dramatic effect, but Levi was trying to apply this knowledge to the creature he had met. At his lack of reaction, she dropped the theatrics and leant back in her chair, crossing her arms. 'We know that when we die, we're going to end up in the spiritual realm and eventually the third realm, just like everyone else. But some hunters feel entitled to something more. I don't know, they think their service to the afterlife means they deserve … heaven, or something? I'm not sure exactly. They just want a reward. Anyway, when they end up as a ghost, they aren't content to just float around like other ghosts. Hunters are always a middleman between the physical and spiritual realms, so even when they die, they're still connected to the physical realm. But these hunters, these demons … just like we can take the essence of ghosts and destroy them, dead hunters can take the souls of the living and claim them. It feeds them, lets them feel alive.'

Levi's head whirled. That was what the swamp creature would have done to Jay if he hadn't intervened. He shuddered at the thought of a hunter, someone dedicated to keeping others safe, becoming a monster that fed on the death of others. Now that he knew this, he didn't want to think about what his side of the deal would be.

'Pretty creepy, right?' Shivan finished off her explanation. 'But like I said, don't freak out about it. We're pretty sure they're just legends to keep us getting too power-hungry. Ghost hunting is usually boring, for the most part.'

Levi felt his hands shaking, and he put down his mug. 'And ... these demons, can they be slain?'

Bianca frowned, her usually inscrutable face creased with concern. 'Are you ok, Levi? You're getting really worked up about this.'

She reached out to touch his arm, and he jumped back, pushing his chair back. He knew they were just more hallucinations, but he could hear whispering. He could feel a slimy hand on his arm. 'I'm fine. This is just ... a lot to process. I should go.'

Shivan and Bianca stood up too, following him as he made his way to the door. 'I'm sorry, man. I shouldn't have dumped so much information on you in one day. Do you still want to come back with your weapon?'

Levi fumbled for his car keys, stumbling out of the doorway. 'Uh, yeah. I'll message you later?'

The whispers followed him all the way out to his car, filling him with dread as stories of demons and sacrifice swirled around in his head.

Chapter Nine

'So, YOU MET HAZEL.' Olive said. She had a few thoughts swirling around her own head. Rita and the boys had told her about hunters, but she didn't know all the details that Levi had just told her. She definitely didn't know that she could kill them, and she wasn't exactly happy to hear that fact. But she had learnt a lot about Hazel.

Levi frowned at her, and she sighed. 'Hazel? You know, the demon? Yeah, that's her name.'

'Oh, so you're familiar with her?' He did not seem very impressed. The whole time he was telling his story, he had been watching her very closely, like he was afraid she would stab him out of nowhere. Somewhere after he finished talking about Jay in the hospital, Olive began to question what she was doing, talking with a hunter. She didn't know if *he* knew what he was doing. By the sounds of it, he was feeling all empowered from his hunting lessons and had decided to confront the first ghost he saw. Not that she was complaining, though. Now she had more information on Hazel, and possibly herself.

'Yeah, I came across her not too long ago. Looks like we've found ourselves in very similar situations,' she smiled, but it wasn't exactly a friendly smile. It didn't matter how many times his friends said he didn't need to slay every ghost – she wasn't going to take that risk. They were enemies, after all.

'You made a deal with … with her? Why? What are you getting out of this?'

Olive smiled coyly, putting one hand on her hip. 'I don't think we know each other well enough yet for me to tell you that.'

Levi was obviously growing frustrated. 'Are you kidding me? I basically just told you my whole life story, what more do you want from me?'

Olive shrugged, grinning mischievously. 'I don't know, what do you want with *me?* You're the one who started this whole interaction, weren't you?'

He narrowed his eyes, giving her a deadpan stare. 'I don't ... really know *what* I was hoping for. I was just trying to figure out who was a ghost, who was a living person and who was just a hallucination. It just kind of worked out that we've both run into, uh, Hazel.' He paused. 'Well, why don't you tell me about yourself, then? Then we'll know each other properly.'

Olive smiled a slow smile, her eyes glittering. 'That's a sweet thought,' she said, toying with him. 'I wish I *could* tell you about myself, but I can't remember! I have no memories at all, I told you that!'

She was being very sarcastic in that moment, trying to piss him off, but he was taking her completely seriously, his face creased with thought. 'Is that ... a normal thing for ghosts?'

She laughed bitterly, tossing her head back. 'Hah! No, I'm a bit of a freak, actually. No one really knows what's going on with me.'

'Is that why you made a deal with Hazel? So that you can get your memories back?'

Olive's smile dropped. She didn't like how quickly he had figured her out. She hadn't meant to reveal that about herself, but it solved the problem of deciding whether to tell him later. Still, she didn't like that he had read her so easily. She kept the humour in her voice, though it had soured considerably. 'That's *very* perceptive of you. Good job.'

He crossed his arms. 'So you want your memories back. What are you doing for her in return?'

Olive huffed. 'I don't know! I haven't actually made a deal with her yet, unlike you!'

'I didn't mean to make a deal!' He said, his temper flaring. Olive felt smugly satisfied, comfortable in knowing she had the power to make him angry. 'She didn't give me much of a choice! I didn't even get time to agree to anything.'

'Well, that's *your* problem, isn't it?' She knew she was being a brat, but she couldn't help it.

He clenched his jaw, giving her a filthy look. He was trying to calm himself down, but it was clear she was getting under his skin. 'Look, we don't have to fight, ok? We're both caught up with this Hazel, neither of us are sure what she wants, so maybe we can help each other. You said you like Jay, right? If you help me, you'll be helping them as well.'

Olive looked to the side. She really hadn't known Jay all that long, but she felt a connection to them anyway. They were so fragile and lost but attached themselves so quickly to the ghosts, and Olive couldn't help but be endeared by them. She felt oddly protective of them, on top of her curiosity about their mutual amnesia.

And then there was the question of Hazel. It seemed like she had stumbled across Levi by accident, but instead of taking both his and Jay's souls, she had kept them alive. It seemed like a waste of time to wait for Levi to slay a ghost when she could have taken his soul right then and there. Levi's encounter with her just opened more questions. Hazel had sought Olive out purposefully. That was no accident. Olive hadn't made any kind of deal with her, yet, but Hazel would still be able to find her. If she wanted to make the same pact with Olive as she had with Levi, then why did she let Olive leave without sealing the deal?

'I'm not making any promises,' Olive said, 'But I'll keep an eye for you if you do the same for me. I'll see if I can find Hazel again and learn a bit more about what her intentions are. If you find out anything interesting … maybe just come back here? Tomorrow morning? I'll find you and we can trade information.'

Levi nodded, still regarding her with caution. 'Sounds good.'

'Hey,' Olive chewed her lip. 'Are you going to tell Jay? About everything? It's up to you, of course, but if their life is on the line, don't they deserve to know?'

He stared at his feet, and his voice went quiet. 'I ... don't know. I think maybe they'd be safer if they didn't know.'

'Isn't that what your mum was thinking? And look how that turned out.' She wasn't trying to bait him anymore, but she thought she had a good point. 'Besides, they're *already* involved. They've been spending time with us. They're learning about the spiritual realm. Whether you like it or not, they're as much a part of this as you are.'

She could see that he was conflicted. He looked like he was going to get angry, but he managed to remain calm. He took a deep sigh. 'I'll think about it. If you see them again tonight, you can't tell them *anything* about hunters, or demons, or anything else. Got it?'

Olive tilted her head, her face a stony mask. 'Whatever you say, boss.'

He gave her one last scrutinising look and stormed off. Dreading whatever conversation she would be having next, Olive turned and began the walk back to the house.

***

'Where have you been all day?' Rita said, rushing into the forest to meet Olive. 'You just disappeared after the cemetery. I was getting worried about you!'

She pulled Olive into a hug and Olive let herself sink into it, feeling comforted by the presence of another ghost, someone like her. 'I'm fine! I told you, I was just going for a walk.'

'Well, it was a long walk. I missed you.' She smiled warmly, holding Olive's face in her hands. She brushed the auburn hair out of her eyes, and then dropped her hands, her face growing serious. 'Marcus is inside. He wants to talk to you.'

Olive froze up. This is what she had been hoping to avoid. 'Oh, no ...'

Rita pressed her fist gently to Olive's arm. 'Don't worry, he's not going to yell at you. You can relax.'

Olive groaned, leaning pathetically against Rita. 'Does he know that I'm sorry?'

Rita pushed her away, laughing, not putting up with her self-pitying act. 'I'm not letting you off the hook, ok? *You* have to apologise; I'm not doing it for you.'

Olive pouted, but she knew she was right. '*Fine.*'

Rita rolled her eyes, but then she smiled sympathetically. 'You got nothing to worry about, hon. He's still your friend. He still loves you. But you hurt him, and you've got to hold yourself accountable. You can do that, right?'

Olive nodded, her gaze flickering around as she half-heartedly looked for an escape route. But she knew Rita was right. She wanted things to be ok with Marcus again. She didn't want to avoid him for another day, let alone the rest of their afterlives.

When she opened the door, Marcus was seated at the tiny kitchen table, his arms crossed and one leg up on the chair. He was hunched in on himself, and he looked smaller than Olive was used to seeing him. He raised his head at the sound of the door, his eyes wide and a little scared. He stood up when the two girls walked into the room, and he and Olive were facing each other once again, but this time the red hot anger was replaced by cold tension, a hesitation so painful Olive could hardly stand it. Rita looked between them, and then silently jerked her thumb in the direction of the stairs and walked up to her room, leaving the two of them alone.

Marcus heaved a heavy sigh. 'Hey, Olive …'

'Let me talk first.' Olive cut him off, holding up a hand. 'I'm sorry, Marcus, I really am. I shouldn't have said what I said. I got fired up, and I wasn't thinking.'

'Nah, that's alright, Olly,' Marcus said, keeping his head low and avoiding looking at her. 'I shouldn't have dumped my whole life story on you like that.'

'What? Hey, look, I'm trying to apologise properly to you here.' She didn't like how quiet he was being, how withdrawn. He usually had so much energy, but now he had almost shut down completely. 'I was in the wrong last night, you know that. I made you bring up all that stuff from your past. *I* was the one being selfish. I wouldn't blame you for not forgiving me.'

Marcus chewed his bottom lip, sighing multiple times as he decided what to say. 'I'm not gonna lie. It really hurt me, what you said. I know you're frustrated with Gaia and your memories. It's just that … sometimes you have a habit of making everything about you. No offense.'

Olive shrugged, giving a tiny smile. 'None taken. I deserved that.'

Marcus almost smiled back. 'Yeah, well ... I guess we're all so caught up in our own shit that we forget other people have things going on, too.'

Olive nodded, slowly. 'I think I'm starting to figure that out.'

'Rita told me where she took you today.' he said, looking out the window. 'She's pretty brave, going back there every year. Sometimes I wish I could go and check on my brother, just make sure he's going ok.'

'What's stopping you?' She said quietly, trying not to sound like she was interrogating him.

He tilted his head back to look up at the ceiling, digging his hands into his pockets. 'I'm scared of what I'll see. I'm scared to find out what I did to him. You know, Rita ... Rita's death was an accident, it was something that happened *to* her, but ... mine was on purpose. Whatever state my brother is in now, however many months or years of therapy he went through, that's all on me. I know I should want to see him, but ...'

'No, I get it.' Olive said. 'I mean ... I'm trying to get it. You don't have to talk about this if you don't want to.'

Marcus nodded gratefully. 'Yeah, think I'm done.'

Olive smiled shyly, rocking back and forth on her feet. 'So ... are we friends again?'

He finally smiled at her, laughing softly. 'Olly, we never stopped being friends. Come here,' he pulled her into a hug.

After they separated, they just stood there in silence. Olive's heart was full. She felt like there was still so much to say, so much to apologise for, but the words wouldn't form.

'Hey, do you think Jay is going to show up again tonight?' He asked after a while.

'Oh, uh, probably.' She hadn't thought about what she was going to say to Jay. She supposed that depended on whether or not Levi told them what he had told her.

'Eh, I guess we'll find out. Zeke and I are gonna wait up for them like we did last night, how about you two?'

'Yeah, that sounds like a plan.'

Marcus grinned at her, clapping her on the back. 'Alright, we'll see you there.'

He left, and Olive breathed a sigh of relief, finally alone with her thoughts. She took a seat at the table and sank into the chair. A few moments passed and Rita came back down the stairs, a cloud of black leather and curls. 'Did you two sort things out? You look exhausted.'

Olive nodded, closing her eyes. 'Mmm hmm. It's been a big day.'

Rita watched her carefully, eyes narrowed but still smiling. 'You're a strange one, Olive, that's for sure. But I'm glad you worked it out with Marcus. He seemed pretty upset by the whole thing.'

Olive opened her eyes. 'Really?'

'Yeah, of course. He couldn't stand thinking that you hated him.'

Olive scoffed. 'He was worried that *I* hated *him?*'

Rita hummed and nodded. 'Yeah, our boy's sensitive. He cares about you a lot.' She stared Olive straight in the eyes. 'We *all* do. You do know that, don't know?'

Olive wrapped her arms around herself, smiling as she nodded. 'Yeah, I know.'

Rita returned the smile. 'Great. That's good. Are we going to wait for Jay again tonight?'

Olive nodded, and they headed out together. Rita had found their mobile phones somewhere amongst the mess in her room and had brought them with her. They spent a couple of minutes seeing what they could do with them, but they gave up when the phones started asking for Wi-Fi passwords.

They didn't have to wait long for Jay. They showed up, beaming brightly, and rushed over. Jay gave a wave to the distance, and Olive saw that the boys were not far behind. Olive didn't even have time to say hello to them, but Marcus shot her a grin and she knew they were ok.

'How are you holding up? How's the hospital?' Rita asked.

'Getting better, for sure!' They responded brightly. 'The hospital's still really boring, but at least I've got you guys to talk to!'

All four of them smiled endearingly. It was very obvious why Levi was so protective of them. Their eyes were so vibrant and innocent, nothing stopping them from expressing just how they felt. If Olive did have a younger sibling, she hoped they were like Jay. She couldn't express how nice it was to feel admired, for someone to be this excited to see her. If this was the face that Levi was greeted with every day, he was luckier than he knew.

'How about your brother?' she blurted, then tried to cover it up. 'And your mother. How are they handling things?'

Olive couldn't be sure, but she thought she saw Jay give her a knowing look. They didn't give anything away with their response, though. 'They're doing alright. Mum's still a bit teary, but ...' they shrugged, trailing off. They didn't need to finish the thought.

Olive tried to meet their eye again, but they kept looking away every time they made eye contact. Then Jay's face lit up. 'Oh! Did you guys bring your phones?'

The five of them spent the better part of the evening messing around with the devices, which Jay called 'ancient'. They grew frustrated with the fact that there was no Wi-Fi in the forest, so they mostly played the pre-downloaded games.

'You won't be able to text anyone, but I could text you!' Jay said as they added everyone's numbers into their contact list. 'Oh, I could *call* you! That should work. Olive, I'll try ringing you.'

The harsh ringtone made Olive jump, which made Marcus laugh. She stuck out her tongue at him and held the phone up to her ear.

'Can you hear me?' Jay asked. Their voice echoed with a tinny reverb through the receiver, making Olive's head spin.

'Sure can! Can you hear me?'

Everyone heard the noise this time. There was a static crackling and the sound of heavy winds blowing. The sound pierced into Olive's temples and made her ears ring. Jay quickly hung up the phone and the noises stopped. They stared at Olive, wide-eyed, and then their face broke out into a grin. 'That's so cool! It's just like in the horror movies!'

This dissolved into a conversation about everyone's favourite horror movies – Jay was an aficionado; Ezekiel hadn't seen any. Everyone else had one or two favourites they could name, except for Olive. She felt that familiar twinge of bitterness at being left out, but she decided that scary movies didn't sound that appealing. Who would want to be scared on purpose?

The ghosts distracted themselves with their phones, testing out all the apps. Jay snuck up to Olive, sitting close to her. They sat twiddling their thumbs while Olive waited patiently for them to speak. 'Levi told me that he talked to you today,'

Olive looked around to see if the others were listening. Rita briefly looked up, seeing the two were having a private conversation, and went back to her game.

'What else did he tell you?' She felt conflicted. She guessed it was good that he was being honest, but she wasn't ready to discuss Hazel yet.

Jay bit their lip, scratching at the cuffs of their jeans. 'He said that he's a hunter. A ghost hunter.' Their eyes went wide again. 'Oh! But he doesn't want to hurt you guys!'

Olive laughed. 'No, I know that. He wouldn't be able to take us. Not with these muscles, anyway.' She flexed her arm, which was mostly just pale chubby flesh.

Jay chuckled, looking less panicked. 'Yeah, I bet he's terrified,' their eyes dropped to the ground, and they grew quiet. 'He doesn't think I should come back here anymore.'

Olive's brow creased. 'What ... what do you mean?'

Jay squirmed, looking uncomfortable. 'I don't know, he thinks it isn't safe or something. I know he's worried about me, but ...'

'He thinks we're going to hurt you.' Olive was hurt by this realisation, though she shouldn't have been. But she thought he understood that they *both* wanted Jay to be safe. Hadn't they agreed on that? 'You *know* that we wouldn't do that, right? We're friends, Jay, why would we want to hurt you?'

'*I* know that!' Jay exclaimed, growing exasperated. 'He's just ... *really* overprotective. It's like, he *just* found out that he's got this responsibility as a hunter, and now he thinks he knows what's best for me.'

By this time the other ghosts were listening to them. Jay grew bashful, drawing their knees to their chest.

Ezekiel cleared his throat. 'Sorry for eavesdropping, but it's really your choice, Jay. By all means, you don't have to keep coming here if you feel unsafe. But it's your decision.'

Jay looked around; their face pressed against the tops of their knees. 'I mean ... I get where he's coming from, but I *like* hanging out with you guys. I've been in the hospital for so long now, there's nothing to do and everyone's just waiting for me to get better. To be *fixed*. I don't get to just relax and have fun. I know I'm going to end up in a wheelchair when I'm well enough to get out of bed and that's *fine,* but ... but here, my legs work! I've got no injuries, there aren't any IV drips in me, I don't need any blood tests ...' they trailed off and sighed. 'I feel safer here than I do in the hospital. Or at least, I feel like myself.'

Olive desperately wanted to hug them, but she knew she would have passed straight through them. 'Well, we're glad that you're here with us. If being here makes you happy, then I don't see why you can't stay! Besides,' she winked at them. 'Your brother doesn't need to know, does he?'

Jay lifted their head a little bit, starting to smile. 'I guess that's true.'

Olive caught a look from Rita that very clearly said *we'll talk about this later,* but she said nothing.

They all said goodbye to Jay as they started fading away. Walking back to their houses, the others rounded on Olive.

Ezekiel sighed, shaking his head softly. 'Really, Olive?'

'What?' she replied with no small degree of petulance. 'What did I do this time?'

'You can't just tell Jay to keep secrets from their brother. That's not up to you.'

Olive frowned. 'Are you serious? He wants Jay to stay away from us! Do you want that?'

The three of them shared a glance that Olive didn't trust. The corners of Marcus's mouth twitched like he was trying not to smile. 'Of course we want to keep hanging out with Jay. But they have a life outside of us. You know that, right?'

Rita reached for her hand, but Olive pulled back. 'We're just worried you might be getting a little too attached. Jay's great, but they're just some kid. You don't really know them.'

Olive recoiled. 'So you've been talking about me behind my back? Great. I guess I don't really know *you* all either.'

She spun on her heel, walking swiftly to get ahead of them. But Rita quickly caught her by her wrist. 'Olive, stop. We're *concerned* about you. You're taking Jay's situation too personally and need to be prepared for Jay to go back to their old life. Permanently.'

Olive hadn't considered that Jay might not come back. She assumed after the second time that every night would be like this.

Rita noted her lack of response, and a horrified frown creased her brow. 'Olive? You ... do want Jay to get better, don't you?'

'What?' Olive took a moment to register what she was implying. '*What?* Of course I do! How could you even think that?'

But it was too late; the thought had snuck itself into her mind. If Jay *didn't* get better ... if they even died, then they could spend all their time in the spirit realm and Olive would finally have a friend who understood her. No, that was a horrible thought. Olive didn't really want that. Did she?

Rita's shoulders slumped in defeat. 'Alright, I'll drop it. Let's go home, ok?'

Olive noticed with a degree of annoyance that the boys had hung back, likely to avoid getting caught in the crossfire. On the other hand, she was happy to avoid them.

They were almost back to the house when Rita turned to face her again. 'Just one more thing and I promise I'll let it go. The way you were talking with Jay, it sounded like you've met their brother before. You would have told me about something like that, right?'

Olive's red-hot anger turned cold. She stared straight past Rita towards the door. 'I don't know what you're talking about.'

Chapter Ten

It had gotten dark by the time she and Rita got home. Rita had gone up to her bedroom. Olive knew that during the night, Rita and the others lay in bed with their eyes closed, letting their thoughts and memories come and go. It was the closest thing they could get to sleeping. Rita had told her that sometimes, she swore she had dreams. It was probably a result of dwelling on her thoughts for hours, but Rita was certain she had seen some sort of visions from her past, jumbled until they didn't make any sense. It didn't sound particularly pleasant, but Olive was still jealous. The only time she slept in her bed was after Gaia gave them their reward for collecting a token, and she could sleep for real. During the nights she stayed up, reading or playing records or drawing. She would always become bored within a few hours, but this was the cycle she was used to. Between finding tokens, which could appear weeks apart, there were great expanses of nothingness. Hours to fill in. Every now and then she would try to pick up a hobby like embroidery or painting, but she would get bored of that, too, and drop it, only to try again when she had run out of ideas for the umpteenth time.

That night, she sat at her desk with her charcoal. She wished it would smudge her fingers. She wished she could look into the vanity mirror and see a reflection. She wished anything would stick to her so that she could know for sure that she was real. She wondered if someone walked into her room right then, would they see an empty chair and a lone stick of charcoal floating over the paper?

She tried to follow Ezekiel's advice and let her thoughts guide her art. She touched the charcoal to the paper and sketched Jay's smiling face, the cold expression in Levi's eyes, Marcus's guitar. She sketched the flowers on Rita's grave. She tried to sketch the dark shadows that had flitted around Hazel, but they were elusive. She couldn't capture their image in her mind, and when she tried to focus on them, she could hear their horrible whispers in her head.

She jumped with a start when she heard something hit her window. It was too dark to see anything, but she had to remember that she was a ghost. If it was just some teenagers checking out an abandoned house on a dare, they wouldn't be able to hurt her.

She heard the now familiar whispers, and with a start she realised that this time, they weren't coming from inside her head but from outside. She got closer to the window, and even in the pitch darkness, she could see the inky black shadows colliding against the glass. Hazel had found her.

She crept quietly down the stairs, hoping that Rita was so engaged in her pseudo sleep that she wouldn't hear the door shut behind her. She was hoping that she wouldn't have to go through the ordeal of the shadows smacking against her until she followed them, but she was sorely disappointed when they descended upon her as soon as she stepped outside.

It was surprisingly useful to have them to guide her that way, because even with the moon shining brightly above her she still had a hard time seeing them. That didn't mean she enjoyed the stinging sensation that happened every time one of them made contact with her skin.

They navigated her through the forest, which looked very different under the deep sapphire of the night sky. The shapes of the trees, some of which were nearly bare already, made intimidating, barely-visible silhouettes against the darkness. Olive could hear the screeching of owls, and then the high keening sound that was a rabbit's dying song. She felt a twist of fear and revulsion as her mind flashed to the rabbit fairy, but she had to calm herself. It hadn't been that long since she had seen that girl, and her ... *condition* couldn't have progressed that far in such a short amount of time.

She followed the shadows as they led her past Marcus and Ezekiel's house, where she saw the reflection of the lake shimmering under the moonlight in the distance. That was when her vision started flickering between the forest and the swamp, just as it had done the last time. She wanted to close her eyes to stop the flashing imagery from dizzying her, but the shadows kept pressing her forward, and she didn't want to accidentally fall into the swamp.

She saw the now familiar bubbles rising up to the surface of the water, and Hazel's slimy, reptilian head emerged.

There was something different about her this time. Her eyes were duller than they were before, and she only came out of the water up to her neck. The sight of her crocodilian eyes was still as unnerving as it was the first time she saw them.

'Have you made a decision?' The hideous scratchy voice wheezed, making Olive's skin crawl.

She hadn't, not yet. Over the last two days, she had had a million thoughts running through her head that she couldn't pin down. She had had barely enough time to process one event before another had sprung up for her to focus on. She knew what Hazel wanted, but to reveal that knowledge would be to reveal her meeting with Levi, and if they were truly in a truce, fragile though it may be, she couldn't betray him by letting Hazel know that they were conspiring together.

Even with the knowledge that Hazel was most likely after a human soul, Olive still was unsure what her decision was. The life of a single person obviously came before her own memories, and yet ...

Olive stared straight into Hazel's eyes, refusing to let herself blink. 'I can't make a decision until I know exactly what it is you're asking me to do.'

Hazel chuckled deeply, the sound rumbling all around them. 'Where's the fun in that?' Seeing that Olive's resolute expression had not wavered, she sighed, sinking lower into the water. 'Very well. I'm sure you are familiar with just how *boring* the afterlife can be. Even with the powers I have gained, it's still a tedious existence, especially for ambitious people like you and I.'

'I am *nothing* like you.' Olive spat, her voice tight. Because deep down, she knew she was tempted by Hazel's offer, and that didn't paint a very flattering picture of who she was as a person.

Hazel grinned sickeningly. 'Oh, child, you have no idea how wrong you are. But why all the contempt? I have been nothing but kind to you, only offering to *help* you, and you insist on being rude to me!'

Hazel was toying with her. This was a game to her, she clearly enjoyed getting inside people's heads. As much as Olive didn't want to give her the satisfaction, she couldn't help a retort. 'Forgive me for being a little wary of a slimy monster coming out of a swamp to offer me power.'

Hazel narrowed her eyes until they were barely visible, and the air seemed to get a little colder. When she spoke, there was no more playful malice in her voice, just disdain. 'That is no way to speak to your elder, child.'

Olive strengthened her resolve and stared straight at her, unblinking, waiting to see who would break first. 'You're the one who brought me here. If you want something, say it, or I can just walk away right now and be done with it.'

Hazel smirked, tilting her ugly head. 'Good luck getting out of here without my help. But you're right, I suppose. I *am* the adult here,' she smiled wider when Olive's eyes narrowed in irritation. 'So I will have to be the diplomatic one. I was telling a story, wasn't I? Where was I?'

Olive rolled her eyes. 'Everything is boring.'

'Ah, yes. And you agree, don't you? It is so frustrating, wasting away the hours devoid of purpose, of meaning. Of course, there is the false life that the spirits can give us, but that never lasts long enough. It doesn't seem fair to have to ask *permission* to feel things, does it? For people like us, it is *never* enough to wait around for others to give us what we want. If you could have that kind of power of your own accord, whenever you wanted it, you would take that chance, wouldn't you?'

Yes. Of course she would. 'That depends.'

Hazel laughed harshly. 'On what? You won't get another offer like this, Olive, that I can promise you.'

'Just tell me what you want from me already, I'm getting sick of this.'

'I invite you to my home and all you do is disrespect me!' her tone was lighter this time, but she was still obviously annoyed. 'Since you're insisting on being so impatient, I'll tell you, but I know for a fact that you won't like it so I will ask you to let me explain before you add your commentary.'

Olive knew she wouldn't like it either, but she was glad that at least Hazel was finally getting to the point.

'I'm sure you're aware, even without your memories, that all matter in this world is finite. It cannot be created or destroyed; it just *is*. And life, the very essence of life itself, is no different. The dead, like us, who can still interact with the physical realm, can obtain life by exchanging it for death.'

'So, killing people.' Olive said dryly. She thought she would have to pretend to be disgusted, since she already knew Hazel's intent, but the revulsion she felt was as real as it could be.

'What did I say about saving your commentary until the end?' Hazel clicked her tongue, and it made a horrible squelching sound. 'It doesn't *have* to be people. You can absorb the life of an animal, as well, but a human's soul will last you longer, make you feel *truly* alive. Now, as for what I need *you* to do ... that *will* involve killing a human.'

She smiled wickedly, and Olive shuddered. 'I am *very* close to having enough power to leave the spiritual plane entirely. This place here, this swamp, I created it myself. It's a sanctuary that other spirits cannot reach unless I invite them, but it is also a prison. I can't leave, and I can only interact with the other realms through my shadows – what remains of the souls I have collected. But there is something that will give me enough power to leave completely. I need the soul of a hunter, and you can give that to me.'

Olive searched through her mind, trying to separate what Hazel had told her last time from what she had heard from Levi. 'A hunter. A ghost hunter?'

Hazel nodded slowly. 'Yes, that's right. That's all I need. Now, I know you might be hesitant to do this, but I want you to think about it. After all, you had your life unjustly torn away from you before your time, so isn't it only fair that someone else be given the same treatment?'

Olive let the words wash over her. She was in deep, and she had to question how much of it was an act to get information, and how much was genuine curiosity. Was she really willing to do this?

She had to keep up the act, if only for a little while longer. Just so that Hazel would let her leave. 'Just … hypothetically, how would I go about getting a soul from someone?'

'Ah, that is a little more complicated than simply killing them. When you kill a living thing, you automatically absorb their soul, but you can learn to preserve it, keeping it safe for me to collect. It will take practice, but when you're ready, I can give you some of my energy to infuse into the hunter's soul, allowing me to absorb it instead.'

'That's what I need to do? Practice killing things so I can harvest their souls?'

'I'd say it's a win-win, wouldn't you? For every creature you kill, you will feel a little more alive. So while I wait for my prize, *your* reward will be ongoing.' Hazel rose out of the water up to her shoulders, and then her webbed hand slowly broke the surface and extended out to Olive. 'Do we have a deal?'

Olive froze. What would happen if she said no? Hazel had obviously sought her out for a reason, so she probably wouldn't take it too well if Olive refused. She knew the fact that she would have to kill not only animals, but a *person*, should have deterred her instantly. But instead of recoiling, Hazel's words were drawing her in.

She didn't want to think of herself as a killer, but … it *wasn't* fair, was it? That she had to die so young and miss out on her life? It would be easier if she started with animals. As long as it was quick and relatively harmless, she wouldn't have to acknowledge their pain. Animals kill each other all the time. And when it came to killing a hunter, well, Levi wasn't the only one, was he? She could shut off her guilt if it was a stranger.

A life for a life. A fair exchange.

Olive held out her hand, wincing as Hazel's slimy arm came closer to her. 'Deal.'

And then everything went black.

***

Olive came back to her senses at the front of the lake, the same place where the boundaries between her world and Hazel's shifted. She didn't want to think on her walk back to the house. She couldn't let herself acknowledge the promise that she made, the temptations that she had given into against her better judgement. It scared her to think that she was capable of such greed, but she couldn't deny what she felt.

She crept up to the house and saw that the lights were still on. Cursing to herself, she paced in a small circle. Knowing she wouldn't be able to put it off forever, she opened the door softly and quietly just in case Rita had gone back upstairs. No luck. Rita was lying on the couch, holding a magazine over her head, which she put down as soon as the door opened a crack and sat upright.

'Where have you been?' Rita looked torn between scolding her and pretending it wasn't a big deal. Looking at her, Olive remembered the trip to the cemetery. Had that only been that morning? It felt like it had been centuries ago.

Olive gazed longing up the stairs, praying for an escape. 'Oh, I just went for a walk. To clear my head, you know.'

Rita's eyebrows drew together with scepticism. 'Another one?'

'Yeah, I mean … we're always inside at night, but why? We don't need to sleep. We could be out looking at the stars all night! It's really lovely in the forest.' She could taste the lies on her tongue, and she hated herself for it.

'Olive, be honest with me,' Rita stood, levelling her gaze at Olive. 'Are you ok? I know things have been rough for you lately, but you're acting really weird.'

'I'm fine!' Olive snapped. 'It's nothing to do with you, ok? I just need some time alone.'

'I'm not havin' a go at you, Olly, I'm actually worried about you! I just want you to be ok.' she moved to put a hand on Olive's shoulder, but Olive pulled away.

'I'll be ok if you just give me some space, alright?'

Rita stepped back, eyes wide. 'Fine. That's fine.' She took a long, exhausted sigh. 'I'm going back to bed. If you need some more *space* in the morning, don't let me hold you back.'

She stormed off, walking past Olive so fast that she almost jumped out of her way. Rita's heavy boots didn't make a sound as she stomped up the stairs, but the hurt and anger in her steps echoed louder than any noise they could have made.

Olive felt her heart sink. She hadn't meant to upset Rita, but maybe pushing her away would be more effective than lying. If Olive distanced herself from the others, she could wander off to meet Levi and, hopefully, practice killing things for Hazel, and no one would suspect her of anything. She hoped that would be the case, anyway.

She went back up to her room, finally, and settled back in at her desk. She picked up her charcoal and sketched crocodilian eyes, slimy hair, and webbed hands.

Chapter Eleven

In the morning, Olive left the house before Rita could rise. She went back to where the market usually took place, but by this time they had packed up the stalls to save them until the next weekend. What remained was a tranquil park now nearly overrun with fallen leaves. There were still a few lingering people walking dogs or sipping takeaway coffee, but it was quiet and peaceful. Despite her annoyed realisation that they hadn't settled on a specific time to meet, Olive didn't have to wait long for Levi to show up.

He was looking over his shoulder constantly, on edge, before he briefly made eye contact with her and carried on with his speedy pace. He hastily settled behind a tall, sturdy tree, out of sight from most of the public. Without looking at Olive, he fished out his phone from his pocket, pretended to dial a number, and held it up to his ear.

'Smart.' Olive said approvingly, and he shot her a quick agitated glare.

'You made a deal with her, didn't you?' He kept his eyes forward as much as he could, even though there was no one watching them. 'I could hear those ... those *whispers* when I got up this morning. I followed them here. I thought they might have been hallucinations, but ...'

He looked her over quickly. 'They're absolutely flocking around you.'

Olive frowned, and then looked around herself. She had a shadow, which was not usual for her. When she looked closer, she saw that it was made up of the dark shapes that signified Hazel's presence. She shuddered and screwed her face up. 'Ew. Yeah, I did make a deal with her.'

'What does she want you to do?'

'Find a soul. Same as you. Doesn't seem like she's too picky.' The lie came easy to her. He didn't need to know that it was a hunter's soul, specifically, and she didn't feel like telling him.

'Can ghosts kill other ghosts?' he asked, and Olive stared at him.

'What are you talking about? Why would you bring that up?'

He raised an eyebrow, staring at her seriously. 'You're going to take the soul from a ghost, right? Someone who's already dead? I mean, that makes sense, doesn't it?'

'Huh. You make a fair point.' She said, pretending to consider it. 'Except, I'm really not sure that I can kill off one of the *only* people I remember interacting with.'

'It's not really killing though, is it? You're just ... setting them free. Helping them move on. They shouldn't be stuck here, anyway.'

Olive laughed bitterly. 'Oh, so you think you're saving them? That's rich. Do the ghosts thank you before you slay them?'

Levi's eyes widened, and he looked a little embarrassed. 'I, uh ... I haven't actually slain a ghost yet.'

Olive burst out laughing. 'Ah, so it's not that easy, is it? Not so easy to "set them free" when you have to look them in the eyes, huh?'

Levi sank to the ground, sliding his back down the trunk of the tree. 'I'm still learning how to use the sword. Shivan and Bianca brought me with them a few times, but I guess I'm not ready yet.'

Olive sat down to face him, crossing her legs. 'So you haven't put Hazel's weird energy light into the sword yet?'

He sighed, shaking his head. 'No. Not yet.' He put his phone down in his lap. 'I think I'm scared, maybe. I know I should want to get this over and done with, so I know for sure that Jay is safe, but ... I really feel like I don't know what I've gotten myself into.' He looked off to the side. 'Why am I telling you this? You don't care.'

'I don't care about *you*, that's true,' she said, her tone growing cold. 'But I care about Jay, believe it or not. By the way, I heard you told them not to come around us anymore. Want to tell me what that's about?'

Levi scowled, looking directly at her for the first time all day. 'I'm trying to protect my family. You can say that you're not going to hurt them as much as you want, but that's not enough reason for me to trust you. *Especially* now that I know you need a soul, too.'

'Are you kidding me? You really think I would hurt Jay? Haven't we been over this already?' Olive snapped, anger rising and boiling in her stomach.

Levi fired up along with her, raising his voice and then quickly lowering it to a harsh whisper as he glanced around the park once again. 'How do I know you wouldn't?

You've only known them for a few nights; am I supposed to believe that you're their *friend* because of that?' He gripped his phone tightly. 'How do I know that you're not just being nice to them so that you can use them?'

Olive scoffed. She knew he was right, but it still hurt. It *didn't* make sense for her to be so fond of Jay after so little time, but she couldn't help it. They were an outsider, just like she was. And the way they had talked about staying in the hospital, it was so much like the way Olive felt in her afterlife. It was the only existence she had ever known, but it felt like a prison.

'You should have heard the way they were talking last night,' Olive muttered, fixing her eyes on him. 'Being in the spiritual realm with us is the only thing that's making them happy. They *need* this. They need to feel like a person, not a patient. And you want to take that *away* from them?'

Levi blinked in surprise, looking like someone had punched him in the stomach. 'They said that to you?'

Olive had found a weak point, and she dug in without thinking. 'Do you think they're happy in that hospital, hearing everyone tell them who they're supposed to be?

Don't you think they're happier with us, where there's no expectations and no one to disappoint?'

Levi gritted his teeth, a confronted look passing across his face. 'I just want them to be safe,' he said in a quiet, thoughtful voice. 'I ... I *can't* bring myself to trust you. But I can't stop them from going to see you.' He looked at her with a pleading expression. 'I just *really* need to believe that you'll take care of them when I can't.'

He had not asked her a question, but she felt like she needed to answer him anyway. 'I don't expect you to trust me. I get it, ok? I don't exactly trust you either.' she sighed. 'Look, maybe the fact that I have no memories makes me get attached to people too easily, but I really *do* like Jay. They're a good kid, and it's kind of refreshing to hang out with someone who's actually alive. It's easy to see why you care about them so much. I *promise* you, I have no intention of hurting them. That's ... pretty much all I can do to convince you, isn't it?'

Levi slouched against the tree with a heavy sigh. 'That's all you can do.'

***

Jay had told Levi they had found the ghosts near the Murphy's farm, so that's where he would go. His meeting with Olive had left him frustrated and annoyed. They hadn't solved anything, and he still couldn't get a read on her. He ran through their conversation again, trying to pick up on any sign that she might be lying, but she was inscrutable. One minute she seemed to care deeply for Jay and the next, she delighted in tormenting him. Were all ghosts this capricious?

Levi quickly ducked back home to retrieve the sword without Nhi noticing. He was meeting Bianca and Shivan for another lesson, and the training was intensifying quickly. Although their ancestral weapons were different to his sword – Shivan had a *katar* blade, and Bianca used a saber forged from Toledo steel – they were both incredibly skilled in different types of conflict, and he was making quick progress despite never having wielded a weapon before.

They didn't take it easy on him, though. Shivan darted around with amazing quickness that made her difficult to see, let alone hit, and Bianca's raw strength made her immovable. As challenging as it was, they made it fun. Levi had forgotten how nice it felt to spend time with people outside his family. He had stopped going to the gym once he moved out of home, and since then he had slowly lost contact with the small number of friends he had. But it felt good to reconnect with Shivan and get to know Bianca better. They were becoming a team, working towards a common goal. They each had their own strengths and covered each other's weaknesses. Levi finally felt like he had something to look forward to.

At first Levi had worried that Nhi would check on the sword, since he had shown so much interest in it after their talk. But he was always careful when taking it in and out of its box, and if Nhi noticed anything amiss, she didn't say anything. She was focusing all of her energy on Jay, cooking them food and buying them comics and books to keep them entertained. She kept a wary eye on Levi, but she was happy that he was spending so much time with Shivan. Between work and school, Levi was able to avoid her fairly easily. He felt a twinge of guilt every time for deceiving her, but as long as she thought he was fine, he was one less thing for her to worry about.

He had taken the sword out now and was practicing a few jabs and swings as he made his way to the farm. His family had spent a lot of time there when he was young, when his dad was still around. It hadn't changed much since then, except there were less animals. He remembered there being pigs and chickens in the past. At least the sheepdog was still there, a wiry collie who looked like he was always grinning. He looked up as Levi came into view, barking hoarsely. His fur was greying a little, and he didn't move with the energy that he used to.

The door to the farmhouse swung open and Mr Murphy stepped out in a defensive stance. He squinted, taking a while to focus on Levi, but when he saw who it was, he waved. 'Is that Levi? Levi Tham?'

Levi returned the wave, quickly slipping the sword through his belt behind his back before stepping up to rest his elbows on the fence. 'Hey, Mr Murphy. How's the farm holding up?'

The farmer hobbled over, and Levi could see that his face had gained more wrinkles since his last visit. 'To be frank with you, it's not doing too well. It's getting harder to manage, since my son took off and now it's just me, and I'm getting on in age a bit.'

'I'm sorry to hear that,' Levi said plainly. He thought there might have been a joke in there somewhere, but he wasn't sure how he should respond. The farm had meant a lot to Levi as a child, so he couldn't imagine how upsetting it would be for Mr Murphy to watch it fall apart.

'How's the family, Levi? How's your mother?'

'They're going well,' Levi lied, feigning brightness. He liked Mr Murphy, but he didn't have time to chat.

'Did you want to come in for a cup of tea? The kettle's just been boiled.'

Levi felt sorry for the old man, all alone in the middle of a forest with a failing farm and animals to feed. But he still had a sword attached to him, and he had business to attend to. 'Sorry, Mr Murphy, I really wish I could.' he said, with a polite sad smile. 'Maybe some other time.'

Mr Murphy frowned, obviously wondering what else Levi could be doing in the woods, but he didn't pry. 'Well, alright then. The door is always open if you and the family want to drop by.'

Levi waited until the farmer had gone back inside before he turned around and pulled out the sword, continuing on his way. When he reached the lake, he could hear faint whispers in the distance, but he kept his head down and strode forward. He saw the familiar log cabin, which had been abandoned for as long as he'd known it, though it had always looked to be in decent condition to him. He wanted to check it out, but he didn't want to get distracted again. Jay had told him they had found the ghosts near the lake, so he kept walking.

The tall, Gothic-style building that had always terrified Levi when he was young slowly appeared from between the oak trees. He was on the right track, but he was beginning to feel a bit stupid. He wasn't even sure if he would *see* the ghosts here. If Olive spent all that time wandering around with the living, why would the others stay put? He had set out into the forest with a goal in mind, but the further he went, the more he lost his nerve. He had thought he had trained enough, but there was a big difference between sparring with your friends and destroying a stranger's soul.

He heard a rustling in the trees behind him and he spun around. He saw a pair of antlers, and then the head of a deer – and, he saw with horror, the body of a human girl. He stumbled backwards, letting out a cry, and the thing twitched its ear; eyes inky-black and unblinking. Two more humanoid figures emerged from behind it. A rabbit-faced girl, her bare arms covered in fur, stood next to the deer, and a fox-faced creature lurked a few metres off, crouching on the ground. The savage animalistic posture of this last ghoul was a horrifying contrast to its human body – Levi fought back the urge to retch.

The mouth of the deer hung open, and without moving its jaws, said in a whispery feminine voice: 'You won't find what you're looking for here.'

Feeling a wave of revulsion and shock take over him, he covered his mouth with his hand and stumbled again, tripping over a fallen branch. He picked himself up as quickly as he could and ran in the opposite direction, towards the old, dilapidated house.

He was too afraid to look over his shoulder to see if they were following him, but he couldn't hear any footsteps. He collapsed against a sturdy oak, trying to catch his breath. The grotesque creatures were gone when he looked up, but he still felt a twinge of horror in his heart that would not stop pounding against his ribcage, like it was trying to break out.

What *were* those things? If he could see them, they must be *some* sort of ghost. Shivan and Bianca hadn't mentioned anything like that in their lessons. He hoped he wouldn't run into them again. The deer and the rabbit were terrifying, but there was something especially malicious about the fox, something less human than the other two that he could sense even through the shroud of darkness that had enveloped it.

He was right up against the side of the house now. He could see the dark paint of the building, the cracks and the lines in the planks. Some of the roof tiles had fallen and were half-buried in the ground, partially overgrown with moss. There was even a broken gargoyle on the ground nearby, one bat-like wing snapped in half. If Levi wasn't still shaking, he would have laughed at how on-the-nose the whole building was.

He heard a noise from inside. The door was opening. He quickly jumped back and pressed himself up against the wall, hearing voices. There were two of them, both men, he thought. One voice was deeper with a Hispanic accent, like Bianca's, and the other was a little higher and softer.

When the voices sounded like they had moved on, Levi slowly looked around the corner of the building. The two figures he saw had to be ghosts, but they looked to him just like a regular couple, holding hands as they walked. The deeper voice belonged to the taller one with dark skin, who had to be Marcus. And the much shorter one with curly hair and olive skin must have been Ezekiel. Levi couldn't make out what they were saying. They were murmuring, heads bent close together.

Levi felt the sword in his hands, heavy and cold. What was his plan here? He could probably take the small one, but he was outnumbered. He tried to remember if Jay had mentioned either of them having powers, and then he realised the full impact of what he was planning to do. These were Jay's friends. Even if he didn't trust their intentions, slaying them would hurt Jay. Did he really want to be responsible for that?

The ghosts didn't have footsteps, but Levi still did. He left his post to start following them, but as soon as he did, he stepped on a pile of dead leaves that made a loud *crunch*, revealing his position to the ghosts, who whirled around instantly. Levi raised his sword in front of him and widened his stance, just like Shivan had taught him.

The tall one held up his hands in an appeasing gesture, and Levi was momentarily taken aback by the softness of his features. 'Hey, pal, why don't you take it easy?'

The short one grabbed his upper arm, staring at Levi through his glasses with thickly lashed eyes. 'Marcus, he's holding a weapon. Look at his eyes. He's a hunter.'

Marcus didn't take his eyes off Levi, but he spoke out of the side of his mouth to Ezekiel. 'I know, I'm trying not to piss him off any more than he already is.'

'I don't want to make this harder than it needs to be ...' Levi wasn't sure where he was going with that, but he dug his feet firmly into the ground.

Ezekiel frowned at him thoughtfully. 'Wait a second. Are you Jay's brother?'

'Oh, shit,' Marcus lowered his hands. 'That's right, they said you were a hunter. That's cool, though, we don't have to fight. Why don't you just put the sword down, and –'

'I'm not here to play games!' Levi snapped, clutching his sword tighter. He hadn't meant to get aggressive, but he was panicking. This was not how he imagined this going. These ghosts weren't creepy spirits, or horrific monsters like the human-animal hybrids he had seen on the way. They were just so *human,* it was putting him off. He felt like a child playing at being a soldier; he was making a fool of himself.

'Easy,' Marcus stepped forward, his expression darkening. He walked towards Levi, towering over him. He got so close that Levi had to crane his neck to look up at him, feeling his face grow warm. The sky grew dark

above them, swollen with rain, and distant rumbles of thunder sounded threateningly. 'I asked nicely. Just drop the sword, or we're going to have a problem.'

Levi was shaking again, and he was sure it was obvious. He clenched his jaw, looking between the two. There was a storm brewing and a harsh wind blowing around them, but only a few metres off, the weather was as calm and mild as it had been all day. Ezekiel's eyes were cold and calculating, ready to strike. Marcus looked like he didn't want to fight, but he was ready to defend if it came to it. But Marcus was right *there.* It would be so easy to just plunge the sword in his chest and be done with it.

Levi tightened his grip, and then loosened, sighing as he slumped forward in defeat. He carefully lowered the sword to the ground and took a step backward.

Marcus crossed his arms over his chest with a satisfied smile. 'See, that wasn't so hard.'

Ezekiel stepped forward until he was almost level with Marcus, but Marcus moved just in front of him so that he was shielding him. 'What exactly were you thinking? You come to *our* house, wielding one of the only weapons in existence that can actually hurt us ... you were planning on slaying us, weren't you?'

Levi's face burned even hotter with shame. He glanced down at the sword and saw Ezekiel jolt forward, but he didn't make a move to touch it. 'I brought that along for my own protection. I *know* you can hurt me. I just wanted to be safe.'

Marcus raised an eyebrow. 'Oh yeah? So what *did* you come here for?'

Levi's eyes flicked back and forth as he tried to come up with a good lie. 'Jay told me they'd been hanging out here. I wanted to check it out for myself, make sure they're safe.'

'Seems like you care about them a lot.' Marcus said. He looked considerably calmer than Ezekiel, who was still staring daggers.

'Of course I do. They're my family. I need them to be safe.'

'And you told them to stay away from us because you think we're dangerous,' Marcus said patiently, with a wry smile.

Levi bristled. 'Uh, I'm pretty sure you just threatened me, so yeah. If I didn't before, I definitely do now.'

Marcus gestured at the sword, looking amused. 'You *did* bring a weapon, so ...'

Levi sighed, rolling his eyes. 'Yeah, I guess I did.'

Ezekiel pushed his glasses up his nose, losing some of the tension in his body. 'You're new at this, aren't you?' He didn't have to wait for Levi to respond, it was clear from the look in his eyes.

'That's ok, we get it. It's ... scary, right? Talking to ghosts? I can't imagine it's easy to talk yourself into killing someone. And you're scared for Jay, too, right? You don't know us. You don't know what our motives are. But we're just people, like you. We're just talking with Jay. We have nothing to gain from hurting them, or you.'

Levi could feel his anger melting away. Now that he wasn't so defensive, Levi noticed that Ezekiel had very kind, gentle brown eyes. Looking into them, he felt calmed. 'You're good at this. Talking.'

He was making himself sound like an idiot. Marcus standing so close to him before had already made him flustered, and now he was just embarrassing himself. But Ezekiel smiled, gazing down, and shrugged modestly. 'I was on my way to being a psychiatrist.'

'Hey, I get why you're so protective of Jay,' Marcus said. 'I had a younger brother. Would've done anything for him. Talking to Jay, it's almost like spending time with him again. It's nice.'

'Yeah, well ...' Levi didn't know what he was doing anymore. He'd had some idea of boldly rushing into the forest and slaying a ghost, saving Jay and ending his deal with Hazel. But that was not a possibility anymore. He didn't want to admit it, but he was beginning to see why Jay liked spending time with them. He could even see how Olive could be likeable in the right situation, when she wasn't being so frustrating.

'So, what now?' Marcus said. 'I'd invite you in for a beer, but you'd be the only one drinking.'

Levi was briefly tempted, but he knew it was a joke. 'Nah, I'd better get going.'

They made some very awkward goodbyes, Ezekiel keeping a subtle eye on the sword.

'Don't worry, I'm not going to stab you when you turn your back.'

Ezekiel scoffed. 'Right, like you'd be able to catch us.'

Levi waited until the ghosts had wandered off a good distance before he knelt and picked up the blade. On his way back, he kept an eye out for the people with animal heads, but he saw nothing.

Chapter Twelve

Olive hung around the park for a while after Levi left. She didn't want to go back home, not yet, not when she was still fighting with Rita. She made herself visible and walked into town, taking solace in the relative peace and quiet there. There were still a few people milling around, but it was mostly deserted. The long stretch of grey pavement and faded paint made the whole town feel washed out, matching her mood.

She walked past the window of a second-hand bookstore, and decided to go in. She needed some new reading material, anyway. She stepped inside, scanning the spines on the shelves and recognising some of the titles from Ezekiel's personal library. She saw something flash out of the corner of her eye, and she turned to the counter to see a glowing token, an amethyst geode being used as a paperweight. She was calculating whether she could bargain with the shopkeeper for it or just take it, when the door swung open and two women walked in.

Olive froze. One of them was small, much shorter than her, and had long purple hair. The other was tall and had a short burgundy bob. As they turned their heads and the sunlight streaming through the window shone on their faces, Olive could see the same blue-green tint in their eyes that Levi had. These were his friends. The hunters.

'Are you sure you just can't buy this from the campus bookstore?' the tall one, Bianca, asked dryly.

The other one, Shivan, was already absorbed in the selection of books, tilting her head to the side and biting her lip as she inspected the shelves. 'I *could,* but that shit's expensive. Besides, I love the way old books smell!'

Bianca chuckled softly. 'God, you're weird.' She looked up and locked eyes with Olive, who immediately turned away, picking up a random book and staring at the blurb on the back cover without taking in any of the words.

'Uh, what was the book you were looking for again?' Bianca's voice was tight and high. She nudged Shivan, still staring at Olive. '*A Christmas Carol?*'

'What? What are you –' Shivan followed her gaze. '*Ohh,* I getcha ... no, I'm pretty sure it was *The Haunting of the Hill.* Maybe *This House is Haunted?*'

Olive rolled her eyes. Couldn't they just slay her already? She wouldn't have thought that hunters would be able to tell she was a ghost when she was in this form, but it looks like she wouldn't be able to avoid them. She slid the book back into its place and swiftly turned to face them, crossing her arms. 'Those books are a waste of time. There's much better stuff out there.'

Both of the girls stared at her incredulously, somehow surprised that she had responded to their thinly-veiled attempts at getting a rise out of her. Bianca raised an eyebrow, staring her down. 'Maybe you'd care to give us some recommendations?'

Olive quickly glanced towards the door. She had an interesting opportunity here. These were two hunters who weren't directly related to Jay. She could kill one of them, and end her deal with Hazel just like that. Sure, she hadn't had any practice preserving souls, or whatever it was Hazel wanted her to do, but it couldn't be that hard. 'Sure. Why don't we grab a coffee and talk about ... *books.*'

The hunters shared a sneaky smile and followed her outside.

'So how did you *know?*' Olive asked, keeping a few paces ahead of them. They caught up quickly, though, flanking her on either side.

'It was pretty easy,' Shivan said, yawning and stretching her arms above her head. 'We can tell you're disguised. You've got a certain ... *glow* about you. It's very becoming.'

She grinned wolfishly, and Olive felt amused *and* embarrassed. She made a curt noise of acknowledgement, turning sharply into a cafe on the corner of the street.

She quickly slipped around behind them as they joined the queue, smiling mischievously. 'I don't pay for strangers. You'll have to buy your own.'

Shivan elbowed Bianca. 'I like this one,'

They ordered cappuccinos while Olive hung back, then they found a small table outside. Olive propped her elbows up on the tabletop, cupping her face with her hands. 'So, I guess you'll be wanting to slay me now?'

Bianca tossed her head back with a sarcastic laugh. 'Hah! Not likely. Not while people can still see you.'

Shivan punched her lightly. 'She's kidding. You're kidding, right?'

Bianca nodded. 'Yeah, I'm kidding. You're flicking through used books, you don't exactly strike me as a threat.'

Olive grinned wide, tilting her head just enough to come off as condescending. 'Oh, you'd be surprised.'

'Nah, I think you're messing with us.' Shivan chirped. 'The uh ... people we deal with usually throw stuff around, make light bulbs explode, y'know, classic stuff! You seem pretty chill.'

'But we *are* prepared, just in case you try to pull something funny.' Bianca clarified in a tone that was much too calm for what she was implying.

'So ... why bother talking to me? Not that I'm not honoured to be in your presence, but I am curious.'

The light, joking atmosphere went dark as Bianca's face grew serious, leaning across the table towards Olive. 'Because we've got a friend, another hunter, who's been talking to a ghost. And you match the description.'

Olive leaned away, trying to keep her face a mask. 'I don't know. I don't make a habit of talking to hunters.'

'Do you know a guy named Levi?' Shivan interjected, her voice much louder and more chirpy than Bianca's interrogating tone. 'Vietnamese, kinda tall, always frowning?'

Olive crossed her legs. 'What does it matter if I do?'

'He's a friend of ours,' Bianca said. 'He found out he was a hunter not long ago, and ... well, he's really throwing himself into the job.'

'He hasn't slain anyone yet. He's holding out for an opportunity though, so ...' Shivan shrugged. 'Consider this a warning, I guess.'

Olive laughed. 'Thanks, but I'm really not worried. He wouldn't be able to slay me, even if he wanted to.'

Bianca raised an eyebrow, seemingly amused. 'Confident, aren't you? Well, I guess it doesn't matter. We just wanted to let you know, but it doesn't make a difference to us what happens to you.'

Olive smiled bitterly, eyes narrowed. 'How kind of you. Are we done here?'

Shivan batted Bianca's arm, impatiently tapping on her coffee cup. 'Can I ask?'

Bianca looked at her with concern, but her expression changed back to guarded scepticism as she stared point-blank at Olive. 'I wouldn't bother. This one isn't very forthcoming.'

Olive sneered. 'Oh, come on! You can't make that kind of judgement that quickly! I'll tell you what you want to know if you stop treating me like a criminal.'

'There's someone I'm looking for.' Shivan blurted out, and Bianca put a protective hand on her arm. 'She looks like me, kind of. But taller, and her hair's brown. Have you seen her?'

Olive frowned. She leaned towards Shivan, lowering her voice. 'She's dead?'

She nodded, apparently unperturbed. Or maybe she was just good at hiding her grief. She didn't seem particularly upset, just impatient, like she was waiting for directions and she was running late. 'My sister. She died ten years ago.'

'I'm sorry to hear that.' She wasn't sure what the right thing to say was. She was literally on the other side of grief, and she probably couldn't say anything without it sounding contrived. 'But I haven't seen her. I only know a couple of other ghosts.'

Bianca slid her hand down to meet Shivan's, but Shivan kept her eyes on Olive, sighing with a sad smile. 'I knew it was a long shot. I just hoped ... you know, maybe she'd still be hanging around.'

'Just because I haven't seen her doesn't mean she's not here.' Olive said, and Bianca shot her a quick look that very clearly said *shut up*.

Shivan tucked her bright hair behind her ear, her thin shoulders rising in a shrug. 'Nah, it's fine. It's probably selfish to want to see her, right? If she's moved on, that's a good thing. I should be happy.'

'You don't have to be happy that your sister's dead.' That was *definitely* the wrong thing to say. 'You're allowed to miss her. It's ok.'

Shivan lowered her eyes, locking her fingers with Bianca's. 'Do you have anyone you're missing?'

Olive froze. The branches in the tree above them started stretching out towards her. She heard whispers all around her, saw shadows encircling the girls, but they didn't seem to notice. She pushed her chair back and sprang up, almost knocking over a coffee cup before Bianca caught it.

'I have to go,' she said with a hoarse voice, turning to sprint and dropping her visibility, letting her body take control and float her back to the forest.

When she was back in familiar territory, she clung to the trunk of a tree. Why hadn't she killed them?! She had a perfect opportunity, and Hazel was *clearly* hinting to her to get the job done. Shivan had thrown her off with that last question, that was all. She'd do better next time.

Although, maybe it was better that she hadn't. No matter how easy she thought it sounded, she would definitely need more practice if she was going to save the soul for Hazel. And by more, she meant any practice at all.

Hazel said she could start with animals. That shouldn't be too hard. This was a forest, there were plenty of animals around. She glanced across the landscape, her eyes picking up some movement on a nearby tree. It was a line of ants crawling single-file up the length of the trunk. Olive wondered if it would work on bugs. Did bugs even have souls? There was only one way to find out, she guessed.

She walked right up to the tree and pressed a finger on the bark, trapping an ant underneath. She pushed down, and felt the bug squish under her skin. She waited, and then a pinprick of hot pain shot up through her fingertip and up her arm.

'Son of a bitch!' she cursed, clutching her finger and kicking the tree in frustration. So that was a no. She looked around for her next target, preferably one with enough brains to have a soul. An easy kill would have been one of the farm animals, but she did not enjoy that idea. She didn't want to hurt domestic animals, that felt wrong, even though she knew that wasn't a fair distinction. Still, she thought it made more sense to kill wild animals. It was nature, animals died all the time. If she didn't kill it, something else would.

She stood still and tried to listen. She wasn't sure how exactly she was going to do this. She had some idea of using her elemental powers, but being able to *find* an animal would be difficult enough. She heard some birds chirping, and focused in on that, letting her senses guide her eyes to where they were. Feeling extremely grateful for the lack of noise she made, she approached their tree and stood under its branches, looking upwards. They were field sparrows.

Olive channelled her energy into the tree, willing a tiny vine-like stick to rise up and wrap around one of the birds. She got close, but both birds flew off quickly. In her adrenaline-fuelled frustration, Olive made the branch snap up to meet them, striking them like a whip. One of them fell, and she quickly willed the branch to restrain the small body to the ground. She had briefly hoped that the impact would have killed it, but it was still alive, its little chest rising and falling with impossibly fast breaths.

'Sorry about this,' she muttered, kneeling down on the ground beside the bird. She had a moment of hesitation, of feeling disgusted by her own actions, but before she could talk herself out of it, she reached out and snapped the poor thing's neck. A second passed, and then a perfect mirror image rose up out of the body, transparent and wispy. It started floating towards her and, remembering what Hazel had said, she panicked and pushed herself backwards, holding up her hands in an attempt to keep it away from her. It hovered in front of her for a few moments, then continued straight until it sunk into her chest, dissolving as it melted with her form.

The rush hit Olive instantly. She felt alive, but this was so much *more* than what Gaia's magic gave her. She could feel her pulse beating all throughout her body. Her vision was heightened, everything seemed more colourful than it had ever been, and all of her senses were more intense than she was used to. She felt jittery. She wanted to move, to run, to eat and drink and feel. It was as if the whole world was hers for the taking. She could hear everything around her, including a mouse scurrying in a hole in the ground.

Feeling giddy with the new energy coursing through her, she lifted up the sharp, twisted root of a tree and thrust it through the mouse's burrow. She felt it pierce through the animal, hearing a brief shriek that cut off abruptly as the life force of the mouse flowed into her. She felt another rush of life, the energy she had gotten from the bird not subsiding but growing.

While she was revelling in this new found ecstasy, she heard the snapping of trees behind her. She whirled around, sending a tangled cord of grass towards the sound. She heard a yelp and then a whimper. She followed the cord, thick as a rope, and she came across the fox fairy, the cord wrapped around her neck, holding her to the ground. Red fur had begun to cover her brown arms. She was growing less human.

Dark shadows flickered around her. Olive shook with rage, kneeling down so that her head was hanging over her.

'Oh, so you're her little spy, are you?' she watched the girl squirm, brown hair splayed across the canine face.

'You've been watching me, haven't you? Keeping tabs on me? I've been doing exactly what she wanted me to do, and let me tell you,' she tightened the cord, her lips twisting into a malicious smile. 'I'm enjoying it. Looks like she sent you as my reward.'

The girl wheezed heavily, mangled noises coming out of her maw. She twisted her body painstakingly until she was on her back, looking right up at Olive. The sounds that she made were barely audible, but Olive could faintly make out what she was trying to say. 'Please.'

Olive tilted her head, regarding the girl before loosening the rope the slightest bit.

The fox girl made some disgusting hacking sounds, the black skin of her lips pulled up to reveal her sharp teeth and dark gums. Her speech was broken, barely forming actual words, more of a growl than a voice. 'Don't ... want to do this. She ... made me.'

'She made you follow me? Why?'

'Said ... she would take my soul ... if I didn't.'

Olive didn't want to feel sorry for her, but she couldn't help it. 'Surely that would be a better existence than ... whatever it is you are now.'

The fox's black eyes grew desperate, widening until Olive could see their whites. 'You don't understand ... you'll be next ... if she doesn't get what she wants ...'

The corner of Olive's upper lip pulled up in a sneer. 'I intend on delivering, don't you worry about that.'

More rustling came from behind, in the direction of the lake. Her impulses taking control, Olive spun around again. The other two fairies were there, watching, wide-eyed as their friend lay quivering on the ground. The rabbit's ears stood straight up, and she hid behind the deer, clutching her shoulder with a clawed hand.

Olive heard movement below her. The fox had broken free of her restraints and was bolting, on all fours, through the forest.

Olive quickly turned back to the other two, who were still staring at her. They never really blinked anyway, but their stares were usually blank and cold. This time, they were full of fear.

'What are you looking at?' Olive snarled, a rush of self-righteous endorphins flooding through her heart. The fairies stumbled over each other for a second and then ran, bounding well out of Olive's reach.

Olive needed to breathe. She could feel her heart racing, making her chest hurt. She sat down in the grass, turning her face to the sky and feeling the faint rays of sunshine against her face.

Chapter Thirteen

By the time she got back to the house, still buzzing with energy, Rita was still out. Olive was glad. She didn't want anything to drag her down from her high right now.

Bemoaning the fact that their house was so empty and boring, she searched through the kitchen for something interesting. In the fridge there was a half-eaten block of chocolate, an apple, and a small wheel of cheese. Olive dug into the chocolate with the intention of devouring everything in sight, but a little voice reminded her that Rita would ask where the food had gone, so she left it at that.

She went to the liquor cabinet next. There was a tiny bottle of Bailey's, which she gulped down. She took sips of the red wine, taking time to smell the fumes.

The door creaked open and Olive put the wine back on the shelf. Would Rita notice anything amiss? How would Olive even explain it if she did? She bounded into the front room, feeling butterflies in her stomach. It wasn't exactly uncomfortable, but it felt strange. Rita gave her a quick nod of acknowledgement when she saw her, but said nothing.

Olive was hurt. She could actually feel blood rushing to her cheeks. She brushed her hair in front of her face in an attempt to hide it. 'Hey, I think we should pick up some more Bailey's for the next time we find a token.'

Rita put down the paper she was carrying on the table and pulled something out of it. It was a conch shell, glowing brightly. She didn't look at Olive, just stared at the shell with half-lidded, bored eyes. 'I already found mine.'

'You went looking without me?' Olive's voice was small, fragile.

Rita frowned, lowering herself into a chair. 'Yeah. We don't have to do everything together. Besides, I thought you wanted some space?'

Olive pouted. She knew she had almost done the same thing, when she spotted the geode in the bookshop, but she was still annoyed that Rita had done it. It meant that she was still mad. Olive plastered on a fake smile, putting a hand on her hip. 'It doesn't matter. I found another token, anyway. Guess I'll just take that one for myself.'

Rita kept her stone-cold expression fixed forward, but then she sighed and slumped into the chair. 'I don't want to be mad at you, Olive. I just want you to be honest with me, ok? I'm trying to look out for you, and –'

She cut off, staring intently at Olive. She stood and approached her, and Olive took a step back. Rita put a hand on Olive's cheek. 'Your face is red. You … you have a temperature.'

Olive swatted her hand away, turning her head to the side. 'I don't know what you're talking about.'

'What is going *on* with you?' Rita grabbed Olive's arm. She tried to pull away, but her grip was too strong. 'You haven't turned in a token yet. You didn't get this from Gaia.'

'Let go of me!'

'How is this possible? Who are you getting this magic from?'

Olive finally ripped her arm away. 'It's none of your business! I'm handling things my own way, ok? You don't need to worry.'

Rita's eyes burned. 'I *am* worried. If this magic isn't coming from Gaia, it's no good. Whoever you've been talking to, they're only going to end up getting you in trouble.'

'How do you know?' Olive yelled, her voice louder than she had intended. 'How do you know Gaia is right? You really think that just because they were the first thing we saw when we died, it means that their intentions are pure?'

'I don't know!' Rita snapped, sparks of flame sputtering around her head. 'We don't know *anything* about this place, but Gaia has taken care of us this long. I don't *trust* them, but I'd sure as hell pick them over anyone else!'

'Why? All they've ever done is give us enough power to keep us coming back to do their bidding! They're not even the most powerful thing *on* this plane!'

The flames disappeared as Rita's expression grew cold. 'Then I'm sure you won't mind me telling them about your new *friend.*'

Olive felt a knot of panic and fury twist around her heart. She screamed at Rita, her voice scratchy with an underlying roar. 'You're not telling them *anything!*'

Rita gasped and stepped back, her eyes wide with a fear that Olive had never seen before. 'Olive ... what the *hell* is happening to you?'

Olive couldn't understand the extent of her panic. Didn't humans' voices usually get husky when they yelled? 'What are you talking about?'

Rita pointed a finger at her. 'You're ... you're *changing*. This isn't you, Olive. Just ... check your reflection, now.'

Frowning, Olive hurried up the stairs to her bedroom. She looked in the vanity mirror, and saw a monster staring back at her. Her mouth hung open in shock, and she could clearly see the oversized fangs hanging from where her canine usually were. She opened her mouth wider, and saw that all of her teeth were sharply pointed, reminding her of the fox fairy's maw as she lay strangled by Olive's rope. Was that what was happening to Olive? Was she becoming one of those hybrid freaks? That's what the fox girl had said to her, wasn't it? 'You'll be next ...'

She couldn't turn her gaze away. This couldn't be happening. She was doing what Hazel had told her to do, and it hadn't been *that* long since she had found a token for Gaia. Surely if that were the case, the other ghosts would also be turning? Her eyes were yellow now, and in her shock she could see a ring of white all around them. She looked like a frightened, feral animal.

She felt a slight pressure on her shoulder. She didn't turn, but she knew it was Rita.

'Whatever's going on with you,' Rita whispered tenderly in her ear. 'I want to help. I want to do what I can, but you *need* to tell me.'

As she watched, the bestial features in her reflection began to fade. Eventually, the reflection did too, and with it, the intense sensation of being alive that Olive had just started to get used to. She shook her head, still facing the mirror. 'I can't.'

Rita sighed deeply. 'I'm sorry that you won't let me help you. I really wish you would.'

She stepped away from Olive, folding her arms and glancing absentmindedly around the room. 'Are you up for meeting the boys and Jay tonight?'

Olive tensed her shoulders, still staring into the now empty mirror. She was waiting for that awful reflection to appear again. 'You can't tell them about any of this.'

'Ezekiel might be able to help with this, you know. He's done some research on spirits, and –'

'No!' Olive yelped. Her voice had returned to normal. 'No. He can't know. *None* of them can know.'

'Ok. Alright, Olly.' Rita said, her voice attempting to sound soothing. 'Are you ready to go?'

Olive nodded, and they headed out. When they had reached their spot in the forest, Ezekiel seemed to notice that something was off with them, but Marcus acted like nothing was amiss.

'We met Jay's brother yesterday,' he said casually, tuning his guitar.

Olive felt her blood run cold. 'What?'

'Yeah. It looked like he was going to try and attack us, but we got him talking and it was fine.'

'Jesus Christ ...' Rita shook her head. 'Trust you to make friends with a hunter.'

Marcus shrugged with a satisfied grin. 'What can I say? I'm a charmer.'

Ezekiel snorted and Rita rolled her eyes, but Olive didn't react. She still couldn't believe that Levi had come out here. He wanted to slay her friends, *Jay's* friends. Maybe she would change her mind about sparing his soul. 'What did he have to say?'

'He's really worried about Jay, which we knew already.' Ezekiel explained. 'I think we managed to convince him that we don't mean them any harm, but who knows? He seemed pretty stubborn, poor guy. He's afraid to lose his family, we can't fault him for that.'

'He's got a lot of guts, coming here to slay a ghost in their own realm.' Olive muttered through gritted teeth.

'That's what I said!' Marcus exclaimed, oblivious to Olive's bitterness. 'He doesn't seem like a bad guy. He's just been thrown in the deep end of things, you know? He doesn't really know what he's doing.'

Jay appeared not long afterwards, and they all settled on the grass as Marcus struck up a tune on his guitar. Jay recognised the song from one of her mum's old CDs and sang along with him. Olive crept closer to Rita, leaning against her so that her head was resting on Rita's shoulder.

'I'm sorry I've been such a pain lately,' she whispered, closing her eyes and wishing she could feel the sun warming her skin.

Rita raised a hand to her hair, running her fingers through the locks. 'I just want you to be ok. I'm really worried about you.'

Olive hummed along to the song playing. 'I know. I really appreciate it. But this is something I have to figure out for myself.'

Rita dropped her hand. 'What if it gets worse, though? If you won't let me tell Gaia, there's no one else who can help you with this. I don't want you to end up like those girls with the animal heads.'

'That's not going to happen to me.' As she said it she knew she didn't believe it, and neither did Rita. 'I'll be fine. Gaia doesn't need to know.'

'This just doesn't feel right to me.' Rita murmured, turning her attention back to the others.

The whole group turned around as they heard footsteps crunching through the trees. Olive was sure it was the fox girl, spying on her again. She let her energy flow into the grass beneath her and readied an attack.

But this silhouette was human. He was a bit taller than average with unruly hair, and he carried a short sword at his side.

'Levi?' Jay's voice was panicked. 'What are you *doing* here?'

Levi scanned the crowd, locking eyes with Olive for a brief moment before looking away.

'You can't be here.' Olive said firmly before he had a chance to speak. They all turned to look at her.

Levi met her gaze without wavering. 'And why not?'

'The only reason you should be here is if you're dead.' Her voice was cold. She saw him flinch. Rita shot her a sharp look and hissed her name.

Jay didn't seem to have heard Olive. They looked angry, hurt and betrayed. 'You followed me here?!'

'You *told* me where this place was!'

'So you took that as an invitation?' Jay groaned in frustration, standing up and pacing back and forth. 'God, I can't *believe* you're spying on me! You don't trust me!'

'It's not *you* I don't trust!' Levi looked around, finally seemed to understand the situation he was in.

Ezekiel stood up, calmly approaching Levi. 'Why don't we all just take a step back and relax, ok? Jay's fine, you can see that. Why don't you take a seat?'

'And maybe drop the sword, too.' Rita said pointedly.

Olive could see a reluctant surrender in his eyes. Either he knew he was outnumbered and wouldn't stand a chance against all of them together, or he realised that a fight wasn't necessary. Whatever the case was, he placed his sword on the ground, but he continued to stand, his arms crossed defensively.

Jay did not look happy with this, rolling their eyes with an exaggerated sigh. 'How did you even get here? You're not dreaming, are you?'

Levi raised an eyebrow. 'No, I walked here. This is a real place. You remember that, right?'

'Shut up.' Jay sniped.

Marcus lay his guitar down gently. 'What happened, Levi? I thought we were cool. What made you change your mind?'

Levi fidgeted uncomfortably where he stood. 'It's … it's not really you guys that I'm worried about. I saw something else out here. I'm not sure how dangerous they are, but I didn't want you out here with no way to defend yourself.'

'You've been here before?!' Jay snapped. 'This is just great!'

'What was it that you saw, Levi?' Ezekiel asked gently, interrupting them before the siblings could get into another argument.

It was amazing, the effect Ezekiel's words had on people. Levi seemed to calm instantly, the tension dropping from his shoulders. 'There were three of them, I think. I know this sounds crazy, but they were people with animal heads. There was a deer, it ... it *spoke* to me.'

Jay's voice got quiet, losing all of their previous rage. 'Are you sure that wasn't a hallucination?'

Levi looked at them with a hurt expression, but he didn't respond straight away. He looked ashamed, like he hadn't considered the possibility until now.

Marcus and Ezekiel shared a glance, and then Ezekiel spoke up. 'No, you weren't imagining it. They're real, but they're not dangerous, as far as we know.'

Jay's brows drew together in a confused frown. 'What exactly are they, though?'

The ghosts looked at each other. The truth about the animal-headed girls was disturbing, and left for some disturbing implications about their own futures. Olive, especially, did not feel like dwelling on them. She gave Jay what she hoped was a reassuring smile. 'They're nothing to worry about. Just another type of ghost, they won't hurt you.'

Levi didn't look convinced. 'How did they get like that, though? And what do they want?'

'What do you mean, what do they want?' Olive said, screwing up her nose. 'They're just hanging around here until it's time for them to leave. They don't *want* anything.'

'But they've got *some* motivation, haven't they?' Levi insisted, his voice becoming more and more persistent. 'Or ... do they know things about this place? Things that you don't?'

Ezekiel tilted his head. 'You seem really upset about this. We know, they're a little ... unsettling, to say the least, but they don't have any agenda. They're not out to hurt you *or* Jay.'

Marcus was watching Levi carefully. 'What did she *say* to you?'

Levi looked surprised by the question. He took a few seconds to process it, and then think of his answer. The effect of a human's voice coming out of the mouth of a deer had shocked him so much that it was difficult to remember what it had said. When he did remember it, he felt a shudder, wishing he had taken stock of it sooner. 'She said, 'you won't find what you're looking for here.''

'What?' Jay looked utterly confounded, glancing around at the ghosts as if waiting for them to offer an answer, but they were all as confused as Jay was.

'Maybe ...' Marcus began, grasping at straws. 'Maybe she just meant that you shouldn't be here, since you're alive.'

'But this place is still a part of the physical realm.' Rita said. 'That wouldn't make any sense. Even if you are a hunter, you still have as much right to be here as anyone else.'

'What were you looking for, exactly? Why did you come here?' Olive wanted him to say it. She wanted Jay to hear him say that he came here to slay one of her friends.

Levi seemed to catch her drift. He gave her a pleading look, but she kept her expression blank. He sighed, lowering his gaze so that he wasn't looking at Jay. 'I came here to try to find a ghost to slay,'

Jay's mouth hung open. They stood up, slowly, curling their hands into fists. 'What did you say?'

Levi looked up to face them, his eyes full of sadness. He took a few steps towards them. 'I was just trying to keep you safe,'

They backed away from him, hurt. Their voice rose in pitch, breaking in places. 'I can't *believe* you! I told you where this place was because I thought you'd be *happy* that I'd found somewhere I can feel *normal!* And you use it to try to *kill* one of my friends?!'

Marcus jumped up, standing next to Levi. 'Jay, it's ok! We worked it out, and everyone's fine, see?'

'*None* of this is fine!' Jay screeched, tears rising in their eyes. 'He's so obsessed with this *hero* act of his that he can't see you all as anything besides a checklist!' They turned their fury on their brother, the tears streaming now. 'You don't know them like I do! You don't get that they're *people,* not monsters, not some empty vessels that you can just destroy and move on!'

Tears of his own were beginning to well, and Levi dug his fingernails into his palms to hold them back. 'I'm not *doing* this for me, Jay, I'm doing it for you.'

Enraged, Jay stormed up and pushed him. It didn't move him very far, but he was shaken by it. 'I never *asked* you to do that! You can't keep treating me like I'm made of glass! This whole *hunter* thing isn't helping anyone besides your own ego!'

This was finally enough to break him. The tears released, and his voice rose to a desperate shout, shaky with sobs.

'You don't understand! It's my fault you're here in the first place, and if I don't do this, you'll die!'

Everything seemed to freeze for a moment. Levi realised what he had said, and with a horrified glance at Olive, took off running through the trees. Jay started shaking, breathing heavily, and then faded away. The remaining ghosts looked around at each other, and then Olive made a decision. She focused her energy into the oak tree that stood just off from them. She pulled on that energy and made the tree fall, severing the space between her and the others. And then she ran.

Chapter Fourteen

With enough energy as she was able to, Olive made leaves swirl out in a cloud behind her, hopefully concealing her from view. She ran as fast as she could to the lake, and when she saw the dark shadowy forms of Hazel's collected souls, she gladly followed them.

She stood by the lake, willing it to become the swamp with all her might. She tapped her foot with nervous energy as the scenery flashed, impatiently cursing the tedious display and checking over her shoulder to make sure she wasn't being followed.

Olive didn't give Hazel time to speak. She didn't even wait for her head to fully emerge from the dingy water.

'What gives?' She demanded. 'You said killing things would make me feel alive for longer than Gaia's magic would. It barely lasted a few hours, and I killed two animals!'

Hazel sighed, a wheezing sound that seemed to fill up the entire swamp. 'You children will never learn anything if you do not practice a little patience first. The life you gain from the living is much too powerful at first, you would not have been able to handle it for more than a night. Besides, did I not tell you that a human's life would be much more nourishing than a bird's?'

So the fox *was* a spy. 'Oh yeah, there's something else you neglected to mention.' Olive continued with a menacing smile. 'I had fangs. And yellow eyes. That wasn't part of our deal.'

The chilling, rumbling laugh sounded from Hazel, making the ground shake. She seemed ... *more*, this time. More powerful, more vibrant. Her presence emanated from every inch of the swamp. 'I'm afraid that if you're going to lose your temper so easily, losing your humanity will only be another side effect. You can control it, like I did, or you can let it consume you, like your little vulpine friend.'

Olive clenched her fists at her side. 'So she was another one of your victims, huh? She was like me.'

Hazel chuckled again. 'No. She was weak, she didn't *want* enough. She wasn't ambitious like us.'

Olive stuck out her chin. 'Oh yeah? What makes me so special?'

The amphibious demon clicked her tongue. 'I can't tell you that until you give me a soul. And you were so close, too! You practically had those two hunters on a plate, and you ran away!'

Olive's hunch had been right. 'You told me I needed to practice.'

'Hmm, that I did. Just a hint,' she stared down at Olive with a disturbing grin. 'It doesn't have to be a *hunter's* soul, necessarily. Anyone in a hunter's bloodline will do.'

Olive felt struck. *Jay.*

Sensing her fear, Hazel smiled smugly to herself. 'Oh yes, you've become quite attached to that poor soul, haven't you? Not that it matters. One way or another, they will join me here.'

Olive felt like her throat was being clogged with cotton. She had wanted to reveal her cards like this, but she needed to know, for Jay's sake, what would become of them.

'What about Levi's deal? You promised to set them free if he gives you a soul. You can't break that promise.'

Hazel laughed like she'd told a great joke. 'That boy is a coward! He would never go through with the job, no matter how much he cares for his sibling. I was just delaying the inevitable by offering him that deal, though it has been amusing to watch.'

'So is this all you brought me here for? To gloat?'

'To give you an escape.' Hazel said with a smirk. 'Keeping secrets from your friends will land you in trouble.'

Olive crossed her arms. 'Well, are we done here? Can I leave?'

Hazel nodded. 'Of course.'

The scenery flashed once again and Olive was by the lake once more. She sank to the ground, pulling out blades of grass in frustration. She didn't need Hazel doing her any favours. And what about Levi? She didn't care about him, but his fate was tied with Jay's. Olive hated to agree with Hazel, but she didn't think he had it in him either. But the longer he delayed, the longer Jay's life was in danger. And since he had just blurted that out for everyone to hear, he would definitely have some explaining to do.

'Olive!'

She turned around at the sound of a familiar voice, and saw Jay running towards her.

'What are you doing here? Didn't you wake up?'

Jay ran in and would have crashed against her in a big hug, but Olive phased right through them and they drew back, looking upset. 'I did. But then I went back to sleep.'

Olive laughed, half in relief and half at the absurdity of the statement. That was such a Jay thing to say.

Jay wasn't laughing, though. Their face was serious, their eyes wide. 'I really need to talk to you.'

Olive stopped laughing. 'What's wrong?'

Jay pushed their hair away from their face, pulling it up by the roots. 'You know how Levi said a bunch of weird shit right before he left? Well, I asked him about it, and he didn't want to talk about it obviously, because he's a stubborn prick, but I kept pushing and telling him that he owed it to me because, I mean, he said I was going to *die*, right? And that's messed up, I should know what's going on with my own life and –'

'Hold on, Jay, take a breath,' Olive cut them off. 'Tell me what he said.'

Jay did what she said, taking a deep audible breath. 'Apparently he made some kind of a pact with a demon?! On the night of the accident. He said that unless he slayed a ghost, the demon would get my soul.'

Their eyes were starting to water up now, and Olive desperately wished she could wipe their tears away. Still, she had to know if Levi had ratted her out. 'Did he say anything else?'

'No,' Jay sniffed, rubbing their eyes. 'Just that he doesn't want to hurt anyone. And that he's really sorry for keeping it from me.'

They didn't say anything for a while, sniffling and trying to hold back sobs. Their voice was croaky, raw. 'I'm *mad* at him. I mean, I should be, right? He's keeping all of these secrets when *my* life is on the line, but that's not fair! I have a right to know, don't I?'

'Of course you do,' Olive said, feeling a creeping sense of guilt over the things she was keeping a secret. But that was different, wasn't it? She wasn't under the same obligations to be truthful to Jay, or even Rita and the other ghosts. She didn't owe them anything.

'So why don't I feel as mad as I should?'

The question took Olive off guard. *She* would be mad, in Jay's place. But then ... she knew what Levi had been through to get to this point. She knew how hard he had fought to keep his family safe. The fact that she couldn't remember her own family made her appreciate Levi's love for his sibling even more.

'Maybe ... maybe because deep down, you understand why he did it? What he did was complicated, but he did it because he really cares about you. You know that, right?'

Jay looked down, chewing at the skin on their knuckles. 'I know ... it's just –'

They gasped. They were starting to fade away again. Fallen leaves started swirling around, picked up by a foreboding breeze.

Jay was hyperventilating, grasping at their own hands and desperately searching for something. 'Olive, wait! Levi said something else – something about his sword! The demon! He gave the demon his sword!'

That was the last thing they left Olive with before they disappeared completely. Olive's mind was ticking over. Hazel's energy was in Levi's sword now. He must be pretty certain about slaying a ghost soon. Was it her? Was he tired enough of her to want to get rid of her once and for all? Or would it be Rita, who he had just met tonight, and could maybe justify killing? Even if she wasn't the one he picked, what would happen to Olive once Levi's job was finished?

She didn't have much time to think about it. The swirling leaves came together to form a towering pillar, and then suddenly she was standing in front of Gaia's tree, with the spirit themselves standing by, and Rita behind them with a guilty look on her face.

Gaia's patchwork wings were raised high, their green eyes flashing underneath their skull of a mask. They bore down on Olive, as tall as the tallest tree in the forest. 'I *told* you to be patient! I told to wait, and you would get the answers you need! And now I find out you've been consorting with other spirits?!'

Olive ignored them. She turned all of her fury onto Rita, who wouldn't look up. 'I can't *believe* you told them! I trusted you!'

A strong wing flashed in front of her face. It hadn't made contact with her, but she felt like she had been slapped. 'Don't look at her! Rita was well within her rights to tell me. I want to know what you were *thinking* when you made a pact with that woman!'

Their voice was almost inaudible through the sounds of angry, buzzing insects that flew all around them in a swarm. They were livid with rage, but Olive wasn't afraid of them. Not anymore. 'I don't need to tell you anything. I don't need you to give me my memories, and I *don't* need you to give me my life back!'

'You think she will give you all these things? You think she'll *help* you?' Gaia's voice was dangerously low. 'She *only* cares about herself. She's only using you, and she'll cast you out as soon as she's done with you.'

'She's given me more than you ever have!'

'Oh, you mean she's taught you how to kill? You think I haven't noticed the innocent creatures you've murdered just so that you can fuel your own greed?'

Rita finally looked up, shock and disbelief in her eyes. 'Olive? Is this true?'

Now it was Olive's turn to look away in shame. Still, she was angry. She felt betrayed. But most of all, she felt trapped. She was already in too deep. She knew Hazel would never let her back out of the deal. She'd have to finish what she started or she'd never be free. 'What do you want from me, then? Am I just here so that you can yell at me? Take your anger out? Why don't you just send me on to the next plane already?'

Gaia's wings lowered slowly, and the wind stopped blowing. 'You don't want that, Olive. I know you still want your memories. I'm ... *angry* with you, yes, but believe it or not, I'm *worried* about you.'

'Why? You don't care about me. You don't care about *any* of us, you're just using us to get your stupid tokens.'

The air grew cold and Gaia's tree-like form started sinking into the ground as they lowered their head in a heavy sigh. 'It was never about the tokens, Olive. It was about protecting you.'

Both Olive and Rita stared at them, confused. They didn't seem to want to talk, the insects on their body scurrying frantically around them. 'If I had let you wander around unsupervised, *she* would have found you straight away. She would have claimed you, and then you would never be able to move on.'

Rita stepped forward, her arms crossed. 'I feel like I'm missing something here. Who exactly is *she?*'

Olive looked away, but Gaia held Rita's gaze. '*She* is Hazel, the demon that Olive made a deal with. She used to be alive. She was a hunter who became obsessed with living after death. I should have known she would try to get to you.'

'But why *me?*' Olive asked, finally voicing the question that had lurked at the back of her mind for days. 'She targeted *me* specifically. She said that I'm like her. Why?'

Gaia's skeletal mask swivelled around to face her, their usually inexpressive face showing great sadness. 'Because she is your kin. Your grandmother.'

Olive gasped, stepping back. 'No ... that's impossible.'

The skull swung from side to side. 'I'm afraid it's not. It's why she was able to find you in the first place, why she knows so much about you. I thought removing your memories would make it more difficult for her to convince you, but ...' their eyes glowed dully with disappointment. 'I was wrong.'

What Gaia was saying made sense, but Olive couldn't believe it. She couldn't be related to that slimy, insidious monster. She didn't want to imagine what kind of person she was with that *thing* as a grandmother. She felt disgusted with herself, and annoyed at not having guessed it before.

Then she was struck with a realisation. 'So ... I'm a hunter too, then? Or at least, descended from one?'

Gaia tilted their head at the decisive tone in her voice. 'Yes, you wouldn't be able to do what she wanted if you weren't.'

Rita took a few steps towards her. 'Olive, what are you thinking? You're not going to do anything stupid, are you?'

Olive brushed her hand away, barely aware of her presence. All of her thoughts were on Jay and Hazel. Her heart and her mind were racing with an intensity that made her dizzy, and she knew what she had to do. Without even looking at Rita, she said; 'With the way I've been going lately? Probably.'

Chapter Fifteen

She backed away from Rita and Gaia and ran, stirring up as many leaves as she could. She heard both of them calling her name, but she kept running, faster than she knew she was capable of. She felt Gaia's magic pull on her, the winds trying to drag her backwards, but she pushed through them. She kept running until Gaia's domain faded into the forest of the physical realm. The lake was in sight. That was the only thing she kept her focus on.

She didn't feel her feet touching the ground anymore. A shadow was following her, not her own, but one made from Hazel's stolen souls. She nearly didn't notice the two figures in the middle of the forest until she nearly crashed into them, but then she heard it. A high, keening, mournful sound, one that she had heard before but ignored.

The rabbit fairy stood with her clawed hands covering her muzzle, barely muffling the scream. She was watching something below her, facing it but walking in a circle around it, trying to keep it at bay. Olive finally stopped running, and she saw what the girl was looking at. It was a small red fox, sleek with a bushy tail. It followed the girl as she circled it, occasionally snapping at her, but mostly looking confused, trapped.

The girl's ears twitched, and she turned to look at Olive. Her eyes were incredibly large, and full of tears. Her screams faded, and then she collapsed onto her knees. Olive rushed to her, keeping the fox in her gaze. She hesitantly put a hand on the girl's shoulder, whose nose was twitching anxiously with every accelerated breath.

'She's gone,' she said in a high, whistling voice. 'She just … she turned completely. That's going to happen to me soon, isn't it? And then –' she broke off into a sob. 'She'll kill me. She doesn't know who I am anymore. She'll kill me and I'll really be dead.'

Olive stared at the fox, which was staring right back, growling and slinking backwards. 'She won't. She won't hurt you.'

The girl suddenly latched on to Olive's arm, her claws digging in so hard it would have bled, had Olive been alive. 'There are hunters here! They'll kill you too!'

Olive pushed her away, standing up to get a look around her. If she still had the life she had gotten from the bird and the mouse, she would be able to tell where they were. Then she noticed the fox again, who seemed like it was trying to decide whether the rabbit girl was food or a threat.

'You need to leave,' she murmured, then whirled back to the rabbit girl. 'Go now! Go!'

The girl gave her one last panicked look, then bolted. The fox went to chase after her, but Olive shot a rope of grass out to wrap around its neck like a leash. It whined, trying to pull away and to chew itself free, but Olive felt no pity for it.

She could hear footsteps in the distance, voices calling out. She couldn't tell who they belonged to or how far away they were. She looked down at the struggling beast coldly. 'You were wrong. I won't end up like you. I won't let her reduce me to this.'

She crouched down, regarding the animal. There was no recognition in its eyes, just a savage panic. She almost felt sorry for it, but then she heard the footsteps grow closer and she went back to business. 'It's too late for you. But you can still be of some use, I guess.'

She reached out to grab the rope of grass, sending her energy through it to tighten it around the fox's neck. She lifted up the rope and slammed her hand down into the ground, snapping the fox's spine with a harsh yelp. The footsteps were drawing closer, but Olive didn't pay them any mind. She watched the soul flow out of the animal, but the shape it took was not that of a fox. This was the girl that Olive had gotten used to, but with all of her vulpine features removed. Her face, twisted in a pained expression, was pretty, but oddly familiar.

Olive heard another piercing scream. Assuming the rabbit girl had returned, she spun around, only to find Shivan looking down at the fox's body, her body hunched over and her mouth agape. She screamed again, this time in anger. Bianca appeared behind her, out of breath. She took in the scene before her and her eyes went wide with shock.

Shivan was fuming, her face contorted with rage. Her gaze snapped towards Olive, and her mouth twisted into a roar. 'That was my *sister!*'

Olive knew she needed to run, but she was rooted to the spot. Shivan lunged towards her, but Bianca grabbed her from behind, holding her back. Shivan struggled to get out of her grasp, but Bianca held her tight. 'Be *careful,* you can't attack her without your weapon!'

Hearing this, Olive noticed the sword in a sheath on Bianca's back. Shivan fumbled, lifting up the hem of her shirt and withdrawing a dagger from her belt. Olive stood up and backed away from the fox. 'I didn't ... I didn't know.'

'You *killed* my sister, you fucking monster!' Shivan screeched, eyes wild.

Bianca still held her, but her expression grew dark. 'She needs to go.'

Olive didn't bother waiting for an explanation. She felt the soul rush into her, and with her newly revived energy, she sped away from the hunters, barely noticing where she was going.

'Olive!'

She heard Rita's voice ring out, and saw her standing there, taking in the sight of the dead fox and the two girls. 'What did you *do?*'

Olive felt her heart twist. 'Rita, you need to get out of there! They'll kill you!'

Shivan laughed harshly, her eyes boring into Olive with burning hatred. 'Why would we bother with *her?* She hasn't done anything wrong!'

Rita walked past the hunters, towards Olive. She extended her hand, a peace offering. 'Olly, come back with me. We'll go back to Gaia and they'll sort this out. We can *fix* this.'

Olive was still a fair distance away. She could see dark flecks beginning to swarm, forming a path to the lake. She could feel her heartbeat in every inch of her body, her head pulsing so loudly she could barely think. Gaia couldn't fix this. Gaia couldn't do anything against Hazel.

She had heard Shivan's heart break in her scream. She saw the cold malice in Bianca's eyes, the sadness and disappointment in Rita's. Her voice stuck in her throat. No one could fix this. But she could stop anyone else getting hurt. She mouthed 'I'm sorry' to anyone who was looking, and followed the dark shadows to the lake.

***

Levi awoke in the middle of the night to the sound of his phone ringing. He scrambled out of bed to answer it before it could wake up his mother. The name flashing on the screen was Bianca's.

'You know what time it is, don't you?' he grumbled, his voice croaky.

'Sorry to interrupt your beauty sleep.' Bianca deadpanned. It sounded like she was outside. 'Can you meet us at Murphy's farm?'

Levi grimaced, not sure if he had heard her properly. 'What, now?'

He heard an irritated sigh. 'Yes, now! Shivan had a dream about it. I told her it didn't mean anything, but she was so sure about it. I couldn't stop her, you know how she gets when she sets her mind on something.'

He certainly did. 'Ok, so why do I have to be there?'

'The dream was about Daya.' Bianca sighed, her voice growing softer. Levi was willing to bet Shivan was in earshot. 'I know what you're thinking, it was just a dream. She's been thinking about Daya a lot lately, it was bound to happen. But I've got a *really* bad feeling about this. Shivan said she felt like Daya was calling to her, waiting for her. But ... I don't know. Something feels very wrong about this. There are ghosts involved. We could use your help.'

Levi wiped the sleep from his eyes, then let his gaze rest on the sword he had laid beside his bed. 'I'll be there.'

He hurried to get dressed, knowing how cold the nights get in the fall. He didn't have a proper sheath for his sword, like Bianca did, so he carried it in his hand. He snuck through the house, desperately trying to be silent as he lifted the car keys from their ceramic dish. He listened carefully, but he didn't hear his mother stir. He took the car all the way to the park, then abandoned it as he entered the forest. He held the sword in one hand, and his phone with the torch turned on in the other. It was not the best position to be in if something were to attack him.

He got to the farm, but there was no one in sight. Even the old dog was still asleep, and didn't stir. He tried to call Bianca, but it just went to voicemail. He tried Shivan, too, but her phone did the same. Cursing under his breath, he kept walking. His mind kept flashing to the deer-headed monster and its cryptic warning, and he felt a chill run up his spine.

Then he heard screaming.

This was not the scream of a victim, of someone afraid for their own life. It was a scream of anger and heartbreak, one that heralded vengeance. He chased after the sound, a million thoughts battering at his mind.

He stormed through the underbrush, through the long expanse of forest. Then he saw shadows, heard voices. There were three figures standing and talking. He was sure that two of them were Shivan and Bianca, but he wasn't sure about the third.

'Where did she go?!' Shivan's voice snapped, hoarse. It was her that the scream had come from. 'Where the hell is she?'

'I swear, I don't know!' The third voice said, and Levi recognised it as the other ghost girl. Rita. 'She's been acting weird, I don't know what's going on with her!'

'Does "acting weird" include killing people?' Came Bianca's dry voice.

Rita seemed stumped. 'She didn't know what she was doing. She couldn't have. She ...' her voice trailed off.

'I don't give a shit what she thought she was doing,' Shivan growled. 'She killed my sister! Are you honestly trying to defend that?'

What? Levi couldn't believe what he was hearing. Olive had killed Daya? But Daya had been dead for years. The realisation dawned on him. Olive had fulfilled her part of her deal with Hazel. He should have slain her while he had the chance.

He stepped out of the shadows, the light from his phone illuminating the three figures. There was something else there, too. A fox, its neck twisted at an unnatural angle, blood seeping out of its mouth. Hadn't he seen a fox around here before? It was a stupid thought. Of course he had. There were plenty of foxes here.

The three women turned to look at him, and Shivan's eyes immediately teared up. She clung to Bianca, weeping into her shoulder while Bianca rubbed her back. Levi surveyed the scene, trying to understand what had happened. Where was Daya?

'What happened here?' He asked, directing his question to Rita but hoping one of the others would answer.

She looked down, swallowing hard. Then with a sigh, she lifted her hand and a soft ball of flame emerged from her palm, floating above them and illuminating the area. Levi put his phone away, giving himself a free hand. 'I don't know, exactly. I wasn't there. But Olive's gotten caught up with someone dangerous, and I think ... I think she's been killing things to make herself feel alive.'

Rita seemed genuinely upset about this, looking at Levi like he could give her answers. But he didn't have anything to say to her. He had no idea that Hazel's deal with Olive involved something so awful. Rita chewed her lip and continued. 'You know how you mentioned those animal-headed spirits? Your friend's sister was one of them.'

'*What.*' Shivan stopped crying. She turned to Levi, her eyes red. 'You've been around these ghosts before? Why didn't you tell us?'

Levi felt the tangle of lies he was embedded in beginning to tighten around him. 'There's no time to explain. We need to find Olive, this ... this person she's working with needs to be stopped before she gets too powerful.'

'Levi? What aren't you telling us?' Bianca shouted, but he was already running. The dark flickering shadows he'd become accustomed to were leading him away, making a trail towards the lake. His mind flashed back to his dream the night he spared Jay from dying. The lake had to be the body of water that he had found himself under. That was where Hazel would be. That was where Olive was headed.

He had no idea if there was even any point to this. If she had already gotten the soul to Hazel, then Hazel might already be too strong. He couldn't think of anything else to do, though. He needed an escape, he couldn't begin to explain how he knew about Hazel or why he had spent time with the ghosts. He was tired of this, of all the secrets, of having to pay off a debt with someone else's life. He couldn't let himself sink to the level that Olive had.

Chapter Sixteen

Olive could still hear their voices when she reached the lake. It sounded like Levi was there too, which was the last thing she needed right now. She was standing by the lake, surrounded on all sides by the shadows of the captured souls, but she wasn't shifting between planes as she had done every other time. The lake remained the same.

Fear and anger blossomed in Olive's chest, and she screamed to the empty space before her, for a moment forgetting that she did not want to reveal her location. 'You can't keep me out *now!* After everything you've made me do!'

As if hearing her protest, the sky began to flicker. But instead of being transported in front of the swamp, she was on top of it. She felt a sickening dizziness every time she flashed from solid ground to a few inches above water, and then in one fluid motion, the water rose up around her and she was underneath the swamp.

She gasped, forgetting that she had no need to breathe, but finding that she was able to, anyway. This was not normal water. No bubbles erupted from her mouth. She was not bobbing up and down as she floated, her movements slowed by the water. Instead, she simply hovered in place. Hazel stood, closer than she had ever been, the dark tendrils of her lower body extended into the water well past where Olive could see. With the life she had taken from Shivan's sister, Olive was able to smell the stench of rot and wet that came from Hazel.

'You're my grandmother.' Looking at the grotesque monster before her, Olive felt nauseous. How could she be related to this thing? And had she always been this cold and malicious, or was it just the years of harvesting souls that had stripped her of any compassion?

The hideous head slowly moved up and down in a nod. 'I was hoping to break the news to you myself, but it seems that a lot of secrets are beginning to spill out. Aren't they?'

'Did I always know I was a hunter?' Olive asked, refusing to look her in the eyes. 'Or did my parents keep it a secret from me, like Levi's?'

'Now, now,' Hazel tutted. 'You've already learnt one secret for free. If you want to know more, you'll have to do something for me.'

Olive did not respond. She was still buzzing with energy, and she didn't want to give away how afraid she was.

Hazel regarded her with a long sigh. 'I am a little disappointed at losing my spy so soon, but I really should have expected nothing less from you. Our family, we're highly driven. We will do *whatever* it takes to get what we want, no matter the cost. I know you'll do what's right.'

She gestured behind her, and the water there lit up with a sickly green-blue light. What was illuminated there made Olive jolt backwards in shock.

It was Jay, eyes closed, suspended in the water by inky black tendrils.

'No!' Olive breathed, feeling all the wind knocked out of her lungs.

Hazel looked bored, gazing off into the distance, as though seeing things that Olive couldn't. 'This could have been so much easier for you, if you hadn't insisted on being so *sentimental*.' She snarled the last word with so much bitterness it made Olive wince. 'But that is the fatal flaw of mortals. You'll soon get over it, once you join me in immortality.'

Olive wanted nothing more than to crush her windpipe, but she knew it wouldn't do any good. She tried to think, to figure out a way to outsmart her. 'But you can't kill Jay. You made a deal with Levi that you wouldn't hurt them.'

Hazel laughed cruelly. 'Oh, but I won't be the one killing them, will I?'

She pressed the palms of her hands together, and a brilliant teal light emanated from them. She spread her hands wide in front of her, and the light became Levi's sword, long and sharp. Olive felt her heart race, and she tried to keep her expression neutral. This was what she had been waiting for, but she had to pretend to be surprised.

'How did you get that?' She asked. She didn't know how, but she thought she could hear footsteps in the distance. That was impossible, though. No one could enter the swamp without Hazel's permission.

'As I said, the boy is a coward, but he's also stupid enough to believe that he's brave.' Hazel lectured, her eyes closed as a smug grin crept up her reptilian mouth. 'He imbued this sword with my energy, thinking he would eventually slay a ghost. I knew he wouldn't, but now the blade is mine. You should have been the one to use it in the first place.' She opened her eyes and stared at Olive with a horribly malicious grin. 'After all, you had no trouble killing a hunter's sibling before.'

Olive clenched her jaw. She knew Hazel was goading her.

'There is another thing the boy will be useful for,' Hazel said, and there was something in the tone of her voice that made Olive look up. The demon was smiling eagerly, her eyes bright, staring off to the side of the swamp. Olive followed her gaze, and she saw a shape through the murky water. It was feeling more and more like they were inside a giant fish bowl instead of a swamp, as Levi's form rushed up towards them, hands empty. He tried to get closer, but it was like he was being stopped by an invisible barrier. He saw what was happening, saw his sibling restrained just like they had been when he saved them from dying the first time. He saw Hazel offering his sword to Olive, and he cried out and started hitting the barrier, trying desperately to break through.

Hazel was staring at him with a look that could only be described as hunger. She turned her neck to look at Olive, making a cracking sound. 'With the soul of a living hunter, you will be well on your way to becoming as powerful as I am now. Of course, you will need more souls to be able to break free of this plane, but it's an excellent start.'

Hazel held the sword out to her in a mocking bow. 'Take it. Kill them both, and be free.'

Olive could hear Levi's fists connecting with whatever was keeping him out. 'Don't do this, Olive! You promised me! You promised me you wouldn't hurt them!'

Olive couldn't look at him. She could already feel tears pricking at her eyes. She knew what she needed to do, but she still needed more time. She reached out in front of her, and Hazel eagerly stretched out her arms. Olive took the sword by the hilt, feeling its weight in her hands. She found her grip easily. It felt natural to hold it, but she took her time, turning it over to look at every angle. She didn't want to let herself do it, but she snuck a glance at Levi. Tears were streaming down his face, and he looked so much like Jay when they had warned her about the sword. That was the last time she had seen them alive and happy. Now they were about to die.

'You're better than this, Olive,' Levi wasn't screaming anymore. His voice was quiet, rough with sobs. 'You told me you cared about them. You're still *human*, Olive! You *know* this is wrong!'

Hazel drifted around behind her, putting a slimy, webbed hand on Olive's shoulder and spinning her so that she was facing Jay, with her back to Levi. Hazel's face drew close to Olive's, and she felt herself shiver.

'Ignore him,' the voice whispered, sickly sweet and croaky. 'At the end of the day, we only have ourselves. What's a little sacrifice in the long run, if it will contribute to the destiny you were always meant to fulfil? You'll forget about them in a few decades.'

Now that Olive was looking directly at Jay, she couldn't avoid them. Couldn't avoid thinking about them, couldn't stop the tears from running down her face. Jay, who was still a kid, still in high school. Who had woken up scared in a hospital with no idea how they got there. How could all of this happen to someone who was so young, so innocent to the world? They had already lost so much.

Olive thought back to the first time they appeared in the forest, confused and convinced the whole thing was a dream. They were so quick to accept the ghosts as friends, and they had looked so frightened when Gaia had appeared and they started fading away.

Every night that they returned, they brought light and energy to the ghosts. The four of them, who had spent so long in an endless cycle of idleness, finally had someone there to break the boredom, to offer them relief. They were a breath of fresh air. They hung on every word, every little detail the ghosts shared, either about the afterlife or their own lives in the past. They were the first living person Olive had interacted with that wasn't just a step on the way to getting a token for Gaia. It made her feel important, to know that someone was looking forward to seeing her.

Everything she had learnt about Jay from Levi strengthened her need to protect them even further. They were like her, struggling without memories, only they weren't selfishly trying to recover their lost years. After everything that Olive had done, she couldn't help but see Jay as a better version of herself. They were so full of personality, so quick to make friends, and they wanted so desperately to spend time with their older brother, who loved them enough to bargain his own soul.

Levi ...

He was still there, but he had stopped thumping against the glass. He looked so sad, so desperate. When she had first met him, she was defensive, determined not to like him. They both thought that they had to be enemies, because of what they were. But that was never true. All that either of them wanted was to be free, and to protect Jay. The lengths Levi had gone to to keep them from harm, only to watch it all crumble. Olive couldn't imagine how much that would hurt. Maybe what he had done, keeping secrets from his friends and family, wasn't the best way to handle things, but what choice did he have? Olive couldn't bring herself to blame him for anything. He was fighting so hard for his sibling, for Jay. Everything he did was for them. But Olive? Olive only fought for herself. Rita was right, she *was* selfish. Everything she did, the bargain with Hazel, keeping it a secret, killing animals, killing a *person* ... she couldn't justify any of the choices she had made.

Levi had stopped calling her name. He looked defeated, but still so heartbroken. Hazel's hand tightened, sliding up to her neck. Olive squirmed under the pressure, and her mind flashed back to the image of the fox lying on the ground, a rope of grass strangling the life from its neck.

'What are you waiting for?' Hazel's hollow, crackly voice whispered harshly in her ear.

There was no coming back from this. Whatever she did here, things would never go back to the way they were. She thought of Ezekiel, who had been trying all this time to help her the only way he knew how, with his comforting words. And Marcus, who was always making everyone else happy but who was hiding so much pain behind his smile. And, of course, Rita. Rita, who had always been there for her. No matter how bratty and painful Olive was, Rita always treated her with patience and kindness, and even when she did scold, Olive always knew it was well deserved. Rita worked so hard to make the afterlife good for Olive, trying to understand what she was going through without her memories. Olive felt a twinge of guilt, knowing the pains Rita had gone to in order to keep her happy. Rita bared her soul to her the day she took her to the cemetery. Olive didn't deserve her kindness. She couldn't even blame Rita for telling Gaia what she had done.

She cared for Olive so much more than she was worthy of. *All* of her friends did. She had hurt them all in so many ways, and she couldn't fix it by sticking around. She didn't know if she could fix everything, but there was one thing she could think to do that might, at least, save one life.

Facing Jay, she lifted the sword above her head with both hands. She heard Levi shout, throwing himself against the barrier again. She focused on the blade and nothing else, trying to shut out Levi and Hazel and Jay. She tightened her grip on the hilt, swung outwards, and then, at the last second, angled the sword towards her and thrust it into her own torso, through her abdomen and up through her ribcage.

'*No!*' The cry that emitted from Hazel was awful, a rumbling roar that was layered with the shrieking of cicadas and the croaking of frogs. The swamp began to flicker, turning dark. Hazel dropped several feet as something seemed to crumble beneath her.

Gasping and heaving, Olive pulled the sword from her body and threw it as far as she could. It travelled further than she thought it would, gliding through the water with ease. She was horrified to see blood on her hand, and she looked down to see the red liquid pouring from the wound. Her body still floating without any movement of her own, she turned to see Levi finally push through the barrier, frozen in place as he took in her bleeding body. She shot a pointed look at the sword and jerked her head towards Hazel. He paused, and then nodded, and Olive turned her attention back to the swamp demon. Her grandmother.

The souls Hazel had stolen were swirling around her in a frenzy. She was shrieking in agony, and then she whirled towards Olive, murder in her eyes. *'What have you done?!'*

The voice was terrible, monstrous, barely recognisable as a voice. But Olive wasn't afraid anymore. She smiled, blood leaking out of her mouth. She hurt, she hurt so badly that she could barely think, but she knew it would be over soon. 'You wanted a hunter's soul, didn't you? You've got one now. You can go.'

Hazel's face contorted with rage, eyes glowing with that same turquoise light that had summoned the sword. She rose up on her tendrils from deep under the water, her hand arched into a claw as she prepared to strike. Olive watched as the silver blade of the sword, Levi's sword, erupted through her torso, a reverse of where it had burst through Olive's skin.

Hazel's movements froze as she uttered a shuddering gasp, and out of her mouth erupted hundreds of black shadowy shapes. Olive ducked to avoid the stream, and when she looked up again, Hazel was disappearing, the same way Jay did each night before they woke up.

Her face went from shocked, to enraged, to defeated before she vanished for good, leaving Levi standing with the blade still extended, his mouth hanging open.

Olive laughed, even though it hurt, and it led to tears. Levi rushed over to her, but then he looked away, up to where Jay was. Olive followed his line of sight. The black tendrils had disappeared, and they were slowly drifting down. Levi stood up and raced over to them, catching them and laying them down in the strange incorporeal space.

Their eyes slowly blinked open. Olive tried to meet their gaze, smiling through blood, and then the scenery started blinking. She closed her eyes. The pain disappeared, and she knew she must be gone. But she kept her eyes closed a while longer, enjoying the peace while it lasted.

'Olive?' A tearful voice made her open them again, and she looked up to see Jay standing over them. They were at the lake, the first few rays of sunlight breaking over the horizon.

Olive got her bearings. She could see Levi hovering nearby, and there were more people. Rita, Ezekiel, Marcus. The hunters. She focused on Jay first, her vision a little blurry. 'Hey, Jay. You're here.'

Jay's face broke into a cheerful grin, covering their mouth with their hands. They started laughing, crying at the same time. 'You saved me! You saved my life!'

Olive shrugged, glad to find that moving didn't cause the pain to come back. 'I didn't do much. Your brother's the real hero.'

She saw Levi smile, then look away. Jay gasped, pointing at Olive's hand, which was blurring at the edges. 'You're going, aren't you? To that other plane?'

Olive put a hand to her abdomen, but she couldn't feel anything resembling a wound. 'Seems like it.'

Levi finally stepped forward, leaving the sword behind. He couldn't look at her, his eyes full of too many emotions. 'I ... thank you, for what you did. I didn't know if ... if you were going to ...'

Olive nodded. 'I know. I had you going for a while though, didn't I? But I *did* make a promise.'

'How can we make it up to you? What you did for them – for us?' Levi said it, but Jay watched expectantly for an answer as well.

Olive could feel herself fading, but it felt pleasant. Like all of her tension and pain was disappearing along with her. 'Just remember me. I don't know, make a memorial or something. Bring me flowers.'

Jay nodded enthusiastically, tears still in their eyes.

'Oh, and Levi?'

'Yeah?'

Olive smiled. 'Take care of them for me.'

Levi looked down at his sibling, but he also glanced at the other ghosts. He nodded, and returned her smile. 'I will.'

The three ghosts took that as their cue to run up to her, enveloping her in a massive group hug that she could barely feel anymore.

'You're free now,' Ezekiel whispered through tears. 'You're going to be ok.'

'We'll miss you, Olly.' said Marcus, his voice wavering.

Olive's throat was clogged with tears. All she could do was smile and nod and hope they understood how much they meant to her.

'I'm sorry, Olive,' Rita's voice was a sob. 'I'm sorry you were going through all this on your own and I couldn't help you.'

'Oh, Rita,' the boys broke away from them, and Olive found her voice. She put her hands on Rita's face, stretching up on her toes to reach. 'You helped me more than you can know.'

Rita pulled her into a tight embrace, and Olive tried to absorb the memory of her leather jacket and her rich dark skin. Rita gasped softly and Olive looked up to see a stream of flower petals surrounding them, pushed by a gentle, familiar breeze. The petals, small and white, swirled around Olive until they were all she could see.

And then she remembered.

She remembered everything at once, all of it coming in a flood so that she could barely pick out individual memories. But there she was, a girl with a family who loved her. With a mother and a father who taught her about being a hunter, but tried to keep her away from that lifestyle for her own safety, just like Levi's mother had done for him. There was Hazel, and as unbelievable as it was, she had been human once. She had not been the kind of grandmother that baked cookies and knitted doilies.

She had been strict and disapproving of her parents' plans for her. She tried to train Olive in secret, moulding her granddaughter to be just like her. Olive was afraid of her, afraid to say no.

But there were happy moments, too. She hadn't had a long-term partner, a romance for the ages like Rita and Carla, but she had had happy relationships with men and women. She took an arts degree and moved to the city. She sold charcoal drawings. She spoke to ghosts, when she could, and drew them, drew their stories.

She went spelunking with a group of friends from college, and the cave collapsed on top of her.

The petals slowly drifted to the ground, and tears dropped from Olive's face, tears that she hadn't felt against her skin. She put up a hand to her face. She could see right through it.

Rita was still standing close to her, but Olive could see Gaia beside her, calm and inscrutable as ever. Though their expression was still hard to read, Olive was sure she could sense melancholy, a touch of bittersweet sadness around them. They extended a skeletal hand towards her. 'Come, Olive. It's time.'

Smiling one last time at Rita, she took the hand. Gaia led her past the others, towards a pillar of white light surrounded by a whirlwind of tiny petals and leaves. Olive saw the two hunters out of the corner of her eye, hanging back from the rest of the crowd, and she stopped. 'Wait,'

Bianca was watching Olive and Gaia, her arm wrapped around Shivan, whose head drooped. She didn't look up, even as Olive approached them.

'I'm sorry, Shivan. I know there is nothing I can say now that will ever make up for what I did to her, to you, but ... If I see your sister wherever I'm going now, I'll tell her that you were looking for her.'

Shivan didn't look up, but she sniffed and nodded.

Olive went back to Gaia. 'Alright, I'm ready now.'

She took the spirit's hand and let them lead her through the pillar, stepping through into the unknown.

Epilogue

THEY DID BUILD A memorial for her. Mostly Levi with a little help from Jay, but even Shivan and Bianca contributed. It was near the lake, a little mound of dirt with a plank of wood sticking out of it, her name carved into it. It wasn't the most elegant marker, but Levi wasn't very artistic. Apparently, that had been Olive's thing.

Levi thought it was cheesy, but Jay had insisted on leaving an olive branch there. It was a good bit of symbolism, they had said. A peace offering, letting her know she was forgiven. On advice from the ghosts, they had also left some charcoal sticks, bird feathers, wine bottles, and, weirdly enough, cassette tapes. It made Levi wish he had gotten to know her better, or at all.

Rita was the one who helped the most. Levi appreciated her presence. She knew Olive better than anyone, could tell him things about her that no one else knew, but she was also the first to acknowledge her flaws. Even amongst these people who had already died, the phenomenon of idealising someone who had passed was still evident. Marcus and Ezekiel told jokes and funny stories, and Jay saw her as their own personal saviour, but Rita saw her for who she was.

'She was stubborn as hell,' she said in her raspy voice one day, when Jay was out of earshot. 'Especially towards the end. She thought she could handle everything by herself.'

She had tilted her head then, smiling knowingly at him. 'Sound familiar?'

But no matter what she said, it was obvious to Levi how much she loved Olive, and how lonely she was now that she was gone.

'She grew me a garden, once.' Rita had recalled, her eyes glowing with a soft, warm light. 'A real garden. One that the living could see. It was her way of apologising for ... well, a lot of things, I guess.'

Her eyes grew cold. 'It's buried now. The rabbits dug it up, ate all the flowers. It was the only bit of life left at the house, and now that's gone too.'

She looked like she was trying to hold back tears, and Levi knew she wouldn't want him to see her cry. He didn't want her to cry either. Even with all of this loss, he still didn't know how to comfort people.

'Jay's still here. They want to be here.'

Rita looked at him again, and this time the smile was warm. 'You're here too, Levi. That counts for more than you know.'

Jay and Levi visited often, packing Jay's wheelchair into the back of Levi's car and enjoying some homemade fudge from the farmer's market on the way. Jay had adjusted to their chair quickly, proud of how strong their arms were getting. They complained whenever Levi tried to push them along, so he gave up.

Jay stopped seeing the ghosts in their dreams. Levi had a feeling that would happen, but he comforted them the best he could when they told him the next morning, crying. They had already lost one friend that night, and Levi didn't want them to lose any others. He took them past Murphy's farm as often as time would allow, translating for the ghosts who were always happy to see them. Slowly but surely, Shivan and Bianca became regular visitors as well. They were an odd group; three ghosts, three hunters and a human, but it worked. Jay was happy, so everyone else was, too.

He gave up hunting ghosts. He decided he had enough to worry about, what with helping Jay recover and keeping his mother sane while also balancing school and work. He still caught up with Shivan and Bianca, though. Their training sessions were too fun to pass up on.

Shivan was unusually quiet for a couple of days after Olive left, grieving the loss of her sister for the second time. But she came out of it with an affinity for foxes. Every time she saw one, she would take it as a blessing, a sign that Daya was watching over her. Levi did the same thing, but with doves, for Olive. They didn't seem like a very Olive kind of animal, but Jay told him that both olive sprigs and doves were associated with Athena, the goddess of wisdom. Levi felt like he and Olive both could have used more wisdom, so it was fitting.

Jay's memories didn't come back, not that they were expecting them to. Jay had accepted it a long time ago, but Levi was finally learning to be ok with it as well.

Eventually, they let him share some of his memories. They treated it like a game, like Levi was telling Jay about a dear friend they'd never met, only Jay would occasionally make comments like 'really? *I* said that?' or 'yeah, that sounds about right'.

Life was strangely relaxed after that. Not entirely happy, as there was plenty of grieving to do, and Levi felt cautious with the knowledge that the other ghosts would eventually fade away, too. But they were all slowly recovering, both the living and the dead. It felt like things were finally slowing down, like they could all just breathe for once.

Levi never forgot what Olive had done, the sacrifice she had made for someone who had been a stranger only a few days ago. He wondered if he would have done the same thing, in her situation. He would like to think he would, but he could never be sure.

All he could do was keep her in his memory and throw petals on the surface of the lake, hoping that would be enough to tell her what she meant to them all.

About the Author

Tahlia Campbell is a queer, disabled writer from rural Australia. Alongside dark fantasy fiction, she writes prose and poetry about her experiences with chronic pain. Her fiction writing has been published in Concrete Queers and #EnbyLife.

She spends her free time playing Dungeons & Dragons, drawing her own characters, and researching obscure bird facts when not working on her small art business, Chronically Crafting.